HOPE AT LAST

HOPE RANCH BOOK 6

ELIZABETH MADDREY

Scripture quoted by permission. Quotations designated (NIV) are from THE HOLY BIBLE: NEW INTERNATIONAL VERSION®. NIV®. Copyright © 1973, 1978, 1984 by Biblica. All rights reserved worldwide.

Cover design by IndieCoverDesign (Lynnette Bonner)

Published in the United States of America by Elizabeth Maddrey. www.ElizabethMaddrey.com

Publisher's Note: This novel is a work of fiction. Names, characters, places, and incidents are either products of the author's imagination or used fictitiously. All characters are fictional, and any similarity to people living or dead is purely coincidental.

1

___

Elise Hewitt stepped onto the narrow trail that led up the mountainside. Would she go all the way to the summit? Maybe, maybe not. She wasn't as limber as she'd been when she was younger. For right now, the plan was to get away from the crowd at the ranch and clear her head. How long that took varied, but her Sunday rambles, as Indigo and Jade had taken to calling them, were at least accepted.

It was the one time each week Elise could let down her guard. Putting on a happy face all the time got exhausting. She wasn't unhappy—not at all. So what was it?

Elise paused and reached out to run her fingers over the smooth, white trunk of an aspen. The trees were different than she'd imagined. Most of New Mexico had ended up being different than she'd pictured—from her in-laws down. Martin— her heart panged—he'd had such a tainted view of life. Elise hadn't realized it until everything had spiraled out of control. Now he was gone, and she was left to deal with the fact that their last words had been angry.

And the fact that she didn't miss him like she should.

What did that say about her?

She started back up the trail, head down as she focused on putting one foot in front of the other. She didn't want to roll her ankle and end up needing one of the kids to come up and rescue her.

How mortifying would that be?

"Don't move."

Elise squeaked and froze as a strange, but handsome, man grabbed her arm. She tried to yank free, but for an older guy, he had a grip of steel.

Her heart hammered in her chest. What was he doing up here? How could she get away? *Oh, Jesus. Help me.*

"Rattler." The man nodded toward the path. "I didn't mean to scare you."

Mouth dry, Elise turned her head and squinted at the path ahead. Sure enough, ten, maybe twenty feet away, there was a snake, starting to coil. She would have seen it, but it probably would have been too late.

"Are you okay?" The man released her arm, his voice gentling. "Would you like some water?"

Elise shook her head and backed up a few slow, shuffling steps. What she wanted was to have more distance between her and that snake. And the man. For all she knew, he was more dangerous than the reptile.

"You sure you're all right?" His blue eyes were steady and piercing.

"Yes. I'm fine. Thank you." Her voice didn't quaver much. She cleared her throat. "I'll be going. You know you're on private property, don't you?"

Little crinkles formed at the corners of his eyes when he smiled. "The Hewitts said I was welcome to explore."

"Ah." It would have been nice to have a heads-up, but they didn't owe her anything. And they probably had no way to know where her hikes took her. Or where their friend—he had to be a friend, didn't he?—was going to wander. "I'll leave you to it."

Elise turned and started back down the path. She only made it a handful of paces before he fell into step beside her.

"I'm Dave Fitzgerald."

"Okay." Why wouldn't he just go? It wasn't as if he'd been sticking to trails in the first place, the way he'd popped out of the trees to warn her about the snake. And okay, sure, she was grateful he had. Elise had half convinced herself that they weren't a major threat. Or that they'd slither off somewhere when they heard her coming. It was why she sang when she walked.

Oh, good grief, she'd been singing.

And he'd heard her.

Heat bloomed on her cheeks. Singing was not one of her spiritual gifts.

Dave chuckled.

Elise glanced over.

He unscrewed the top of a canteen and offered it. "You sure you don't want some water? You look a little peaky."

Elise huffed out a breath. "I'm not peaky, and I have my own water. Thank you."

He nodded once and took a long drink himself before screwing the cap back on. "So you live at Hope Ranch?"

"Yes." And at this rate, she couldn't wait to get back to it. Maybe hiking on her own was a bad plan after all. She patted the pocket where her cell phone was tucked. There wasn't a reliable signal up here, but if she kept going down toward the ranch, it was only going to get stronger.

"Not much on talking, are you?"

She shot him a tight smile. Why wouldn't he just go away?

"Never understood that, myself. There's always something to learn when you meet new people. Always interesting, too, to see the way God's been working in their lives. Then again, I've never minded carrying the bulk of the conversation. I can usually find something to talk about."

Elise snorted. She couldn't stop herself.

Dave just laughed. "It's true, so I don't see the point in trying to deny it. You see many rattlers like that one back there?"

Elise suppressed a shudder and shook her head.

"I imagine they usually make themselves scarce when people are around. Wonder what was up with that one. You weren't exactly sneaking."

Heat flooded her face again and she stopped, planting her hands on her hips. "Are you complaining about my singing?"

"Not at all. It's what made me change course. I wondered who was out here doing hymn mashups."

Elise turned and looked away from his captivating gaze. "I can never remember all the words. I figure God probably doesn't mind if I make my own medley."

"I imagine you're right."

She glanced back at him. Was he making fun? He didn't look like it. Elise unslung her backpack and tugged out her water bottle. She took a quick drink before packing it away and starting back toward the ranch.

"Still. I guess it was good I heard you. Would you have seen it, do you think? The snake?" He was hiking easily beside her, even though she'd picked up her pace to where she was almost out of breath.

Why was he still following her?

"I guess we'll never know."

He grinned. "True enough. I haven't seen a lot of rattlesnakes in my life. Other kinds, sure—you spend much time in Africa and Asia and you're bound to encounter plenty of things that would just as soon kill you as be your friend. Mostly, they leave you alone if you steer clear."

Who was this man?

Something in her expression must have let him know she found him odd.

He chuckled again—the man certainly laughed easily—and tucked his hands in his pockets. "I guess you don't keep up with the camp the Hewitts have?"

She frowned. What did that have to do with anything?

He pointed his thumb toward his chest. "I'm going to be running some groups there this month and next."

"You're the missionary?" She blurted out the words before she was able to stop them. He didn't look anything like her mental image of a missionary. Of course, her experience with that profession was limited. Even still, a fit, handsome man was never going to have occurred to her.

He grinned. "That I am. Or was. I guess I can't technically say I'm still a missionary, though I do help out the agency still. They said I'm too old to go back full time."

"Too old?" He didn't look much older than she was. "You don't seem old enough to be retired."

"Thanks. I probably could have pushed—but when my wife passed, I needed some time to recover. When I was ready, they had other plans." He shrugged. "I kind of like the variety, if I'm honest."

"I'm sorry for your loss."

He smiled, but it didn't quite reach his eyes. "Now that you know all about me, do I get to know your name?"

Elise paused. They'd reached the edge of the forest. Now, the path led them out into the meadow where the ranch was situated. She hadn't had much of a hike. And it certainly hadn't been the quiet, solo time she looked forward to every week. But it had still been strangely relaxing. She turned to study Dave before nodding and offering her hand. "I'm Elise Hewitt."

His hand was warm and his grip firm. There were calluses,

but aside from them, his skin was smooth. If her hand tingled when he held it in his, Elise would chalk it up to lack of oxygen from walking too quickly back down the slope.

She tugged her hand loose. "Nice to meet you."

"The pleasure's mine. You live here at the ranch? You're a Hewitt. You must."

"I do. And I should actually be getting back." Elise cleared her throat and fought the urge to cross her arms. "I hope your camps are successful."

He tilted his head to the side, one corner of his mouth quirking up. "I'm sure they will be. I guess I'll see you around."

She didn't bother to correct him. Elise offered one more tight smile before heading back toward her cabin. If she wanted to be alone in the future, she'd just stay there. Jade didn't work on Sundays, so she wouldn't be in to use the office space they'd set up for her in the second bedroom. And that was the only time Elise had company.

She saw plenty of her kids—she wasn't lonely.

Much.

She sighed and slowed her steps. She was probably far enough from that man—Dave—that she could take a more leisurely pace. She breathed in the summer scents that wafted on the light breeze. Maybe she should just walk around the ranch instead of wandering off into the forest and up. But she liked the views from the top—or even the clearing where they went to watch fireworks on the 4th of July. There was something about looking out over God's creation that made her feel small but important at the same time.

It still amazed her that God wanted anything to do with her.

She hadn't come to Him young when He could use her for great things throughout her life. No. She'd only recently realized her need for God—and as much as she needed Him, what could He possibly want with her? She was fifty-three years old. Her kids were grown and married—and wasn't that a blessing? Although some of them had taken less conventional routes to the altar, they were all now married and following Jesus. She had five grandchildren, if she counted Jade's stepdaughter. Which she did.

Even counting Jade was a big step for Elise, but it was the right one. She might not be related to Jade by blood, but the girl was Martin's, and that made her Elise's, too.

She smiled slightly. That attitude was a switch, as well. Something only her new relationship with Jesus would ever have accomplished.

"You're back early."

Elise glanced over at her daughter Indigo and smiled. Her granddaughter, another Elise, toddled on the porch of the cabin Indigo and her husband Joaquin shared. Elise adjusted her path and headed over.

Indigo unlatched the baby gate they'd added to make the porch a safe outdoor space for the toddler. "Something happen?"

"No." Elise grimaced. "Well, maybe. I ran into the man who's running those missionary experiences over at the camp."

"He's here already? I would've expected Skye to say something if she had people at the lodge." Indigo shrugged and gestured to the porch swing, another newish addition to the space. "Care to join me?"

"Sure." Elise sat and gave the swing a little push. She and Indigo drifted back and forth while the baby jabbered at her toys and ran around.

"Do I need to ask if something happened again? You're quiet."

"No. Not like you mean. He seems nice enough. He's a talker."

Indigo laughed. "I know how you love those."

"Especially when I'm trying to have some quiet time to myself." Elise smiled and shook her head. "It wasn't all that unpleasant. And he saved me from stepping on a rattlesnake. So that's a plus."

"Mom." Indigo grabbed her hand. "Are you okay? You're sure you weren't near enough—"

"Relax." Elise patted Indigo's arm. "I was nowhere near it. And I was singing—I'm surprised it stuck around, honestly. I probably would have seen it before I stepped on it."

Indigo snorted. "I'm glad he was there."

"It does have me rethinking my Sunday rambles a little. I don't know." Elise was loath to give up her hikes. She enjoyed the time to herself. And the exercise. "I guess we'll see."

"And you're going to tell me not to worry, right?"

Elise slanted a look at her daughter. "Well, let's see. You took off at nineteen to go live in an artist commune and raise sheep and alpacas with a man you'd known for ten minutes."

Indigo laughed. "It was a little longer than ten minutes."

"Fine. Six weeks. And I heard from you, what? Two, three times a year?"

Indigo's sigh was heavy but she held up both hands. "All right. All right. You're an adult who's capable of running her own life. Just like I was then."

"You still are today. In fact, I think you're doing a marvelous job." Elise paused to watch her namesake pick up a teddy bear, brush it off, and give it a sloppy kiss before aiming her chubby legs toward them. "You're a fabulous mother."

Indigo took the teddy when it was offered. "Thanks, baby." She turned to look at her mother, her eyes shining. "Thanks. I want to be good at it. I didn't know it was possible to want something that much."

Elise rubbed Indigo's arm, hoping to provide reassurance. It was rare to see Indigo anything other than confident. "Hard to believe she'll be a year old soon."

"Five days." Indigo sniffed and wiped her eyes. "Our anniversary and her birthday on the same day. I was thinking I'd like to have a party. We never did really get to that wedding reception you planned."

"True. I think that's a great idea. Have you talked to Maria?"

"Oh, Mom. It's too late, isn't it? She can't—"

"I wouldn't count her out just yet. At least ask her. She can say no." Maria, her oldest son's wife, was the ranch chef. There wasn't going to be a catering option that could do better. The only leg up a restaurant might have would be staff. But if Maria said she could do it, she'd pull off something amazing.

"Can you watch Elise? Maybe I'll just dash over there and chat with her about it now."

"Of course. Where's Joaquin?"

Indigo rolled her eyes. "Napping."

Elise chuckled. Martin had been a fan of the Sunday nap, too. She fought the sadness that tinged the memory. Everything about her relationship with Martin was a mass of mixed emotions. They'd had good years together, but she couldn't look back on them and say they'd been happy. Not truly. Then again, happiness like that was only for movies and novels. Real life? Well, it always intruded. "I'll keep an eye on her. In fact, why don't I take her back to my cabin? Then, when you're done talking to Maria about your party, you can go get a little Sunday afternoon nap of your own."

"Mom."

"What?" Elise schooled her features into an expression she hoped looked innocent. "Dads aren't the only ones who need sleep."

Indigo studied Elise before nodding. "All right. Thanks. If she starts to get cranky—"

"I'll remember that I raised five kids of my own and take care of it. Go. Otherwise you'll miss out on that nap." Elise stood and collected a handful of toys before approaching her granddaughter. "Want to come to Nan's for a bit, Lissy?"

"Nananana!" Chubby fingers curled around Elise's and warmth of love filled her heart. It was similar to the sensation of holding Dave's hand. Not that she'd held his hand. They'd greeted each other like civilized people, was all. And there was nothing special about his touch. There just weren't many opportunities for Elise to interact that way with people these days.

It certainly wasn't chemistry. Not at her age.

That would be ridiculous.

"Come on, baby girl. I'm in the mood for a cookie."

"Cookie!"

"Mom."

"Oh, Indigo, shush. Nan's privilege."

Indigo shook her head, but she smiled as she unlatched the baby gate to let them down from the porch. "Be good for Nan, lovebug."

"Cookie!"

"I've got this." Elise tugged up on the baby's arm as she started to stumble. "Just swing by when you're done with your nap."

2

Dave Fitzgerald whistled as he weaved between the trunks of aspens and ponderosa pines that made up the bulk of the forest on the Hewitts' ranch. He'd spent a lot of time emailing and chatting with Wayne Hewitt as he prepped for the two months he'd be here. Dave already felt like he and Wayne were lifelong friends. Hopefully, he'd get to meet him in person before too long.

He hadn't planned to get to the ranch so early, but the campground he'd chosen the night before had been beside a train track and the two-a.m. freight special that zoomed by blowing its whistle had decided for him. When no one had answered at the lodge, he'd parked and gone off to ramble. Wayne had said he could use whatever part of the property wasn't actively needed by the ranch—and maybe the man had meant after Dave had officially checked in, but he hadn't said that. A hike never hurt anyone.

Unless that someone stepped on a snake.

The image of Elise Hewitt formed in his head, and he didn't bother to try and stop his smile. Bumping into her had been a nice little interlude. She hadn't really wanted him to walk down with her. He'd picked up on that, but he hadn't been sure she should go on her own. What if there were other snakes?

She hadn't been wearing a ring.

Not that he was looking. He wasn't. It was just something he noticed. She looked to be about his age, maybe a little younger. It might be nice to have someone to talk to who wasn't one of his charges.

He stepped out from between the trees and onto the dirt road that led back to the parking area in front of the lodge. Dave paid more attention this time to what he passed as he wandered. He hadn't noticed the archery range when he first walked past—he'd been intent on the forest and the slope of the mountain ahead.

Would the camp have equipment they could use? Proficiency with a bow was never a bad thing. He could work it into some of the circuits.

His feet crunched gravel as he moved from the road to the parking area. There were two other cars there now. Maybe he could check in and get a tour. He probably wouldn't end up using the camp facilities, or at least not often. Part of the purpose was to give people a taste of living without technology and modern conveniences. There was no running water in the jungles of Papua New Guinea. Unless the river counted.

He chuckled to himself as he climbed the steps to the lodge.

A lovely young woman stepped out onto the porch, her phone to her ear. She stopped and a hint of a frown creased her forehead. "Hang on, Grandpa. Let me call you back."

She ended the call and sent him a suspicious glance. "Can I help you?"

"If you're Skye Young then yes, you can. I'm Dave Fitzgerald. I hope you're expecting me." He smiled. Were all the women at Hope Ranch nervy like this? Elise had been. Now this young lady. Maybe it was him.

"Mr. Fitzgerald, hi. Welcome. We weren't expecting you until closer to dinner." Skye crossed the porch and extended her hand. "Is that your car?"

"It is. Yes. Sorry. I guess I should have called when my plans changed." He gave her hand a quick squeeze. "No one was home when I arrived, so I went for a bit of a hike."

"That's fine. It really is. We've had a little trouble with local kids leaving their cars and sneaking into the woods." Skye shook her head. "So when we see an unknown car, we've started acting faster. So far no one's been hurt on our property, but it only takes one to cause a bunch of problems."

Dave nodded. Liability was an issue for everyone. It was one of the reasons his usual location for these roughing-it sessions had fallen through. They were shutting down—unwilling or unable to continue to carry the necessary insurance to make it possible. "I'm sorry."

"Please, it's fine. I'm glad you arrived safely. Would you like the tour?" Skye gestured to the lodge and beckoned for him to follow her. "Let me just call Grandpa back and tell him everything is okay. My husband, Morgan, is through there fixing a snack. Have you had lunch?"

"Not yet." He'd had a granola bar while he was hiking, but he could do with more.

"You're welcome to whatever you can find in the kitchen—it's pretty well stocked. The cook won't be here for your groups until Wednesday, like you requested."

He nodded. She didn't look like she understood why he'd set it up that way, but she was too polite to ask. "Thanks. I'll go see what I can rustle up."

Dave headed into the lodge, glancing around at the large foyer and gathering space. It would be good for breakouts and quiet times. It probably wasn't posh by modern standards, but compared to what he was used to, it was five stars. He followed the sounds of food preparation and found the kitchen. It was a good space—gleaming stainless steel everywhere—and the man standing at one of the counters offered an easy grin.

"Hiya."

"Hello. I'm Dave."

"Morgan." He wiped his hand on his jeans before offering it.

Dave chuckled and returned the handshake. "Your wife said I could fix myself some lunch?"

"Absolutely. Make yourself at home. I've been fascinated reading up on what you're going to do here. It feels like there'd be easier ways to see if someone was suited for mission work."

Dave shrugged as he started opening cabinets. He found bread and peanut butter. A glance in the fridge revealed strawberry jelly. That would do it. "You're thinking a short-term mission trip?"

"I guess, yeah. Every church in America seems to have a sister church in another country these days. The youth all go for spring break and teach VBS or paint houses. Isn't that the same thing?"

"It can be similar." Dave took three slices of bread out of the bag. He didn't need two full sandwiches, but one wouldn't quite be enough. One and a half it was. "But most of the time, you stay in relative luxury when you're on a short-term trip. The hosting church makes room in their building, if they have one, or they put you up in the homes of their congregation. Depending on where you get sent full time, you might have even nicer accommodations—your own house or apartment, for example, if you're going to more settled countries. But you could end up called to any of the unreached tribes around the world, and then you'll be blessed indeed if you even get a grass roof over your head for the first little while before they accept you."

"Okay. That makes sense. I guess they're not sending youth groups into the jungle."

Dave laughed as he sliced one piece of bread in half and then began to spread the peanut butter. "Not usually, no."

"So are all these campers thinking they'd like an assignment like that?" Morgan dipped chips in the small bowl of salsa he'd poured.

"It's more accurate to say they're not opposed to it. So we give them a chance to experience a little of what it might be like and to spend time praying for God to make their calling clear. At the end of the day, we want people to go where God is leading." Dave finished smearing jelly over the top of the peanut butter before he screwed the lid back on the jelly jar and flipped the top pieces of bread over onto the sandwiches.

"That's best for anyone—missionary or not."

Dave nodded. His mouth was full of sticky peanut butter and bread. Was there anything more satisfying than a PB&J? Maybe normal people didn't get rapturous over plain fare, but he inevitably missed these when he was spending a couple of months in a row roasting whatever he could hunt on a spit over a fire. Sometimes it tasted okay. But not usually. Mary'd had a way with seasoning. Even in the jungle. Or maybe he hadn't noticed as much because whatever she made was fixed with love. He missed that.

"When do the campers come?" Morgan finished off the little bowl of salsa and carried his dishes to the sink. He rinsed them and added them to the dishwasher.

"Wednesday." Dave pointed at the fridge. "Is there milk in there?"

"Yeah. Can I get you a glass?"

"Please." Dave watched and made mental notes for where they kept things, as Morgan moved around the kitchen. The cook would handle the bulk of food prep when they were using the lodge, but it was never a bad plan to know where to look when a snack attack happened. "If I recall from my chats with Wayne, you're the horse wrangler?"

Morgan laughed. "That's right. We're not so fancy with titles. I just say I hang out in the stable."

"You think we could arrange to do a trail ride?"

"Sure. Is that a missionary thing?"

"I guess it could be, but I wasn't thinking of it like that. It's fun and would be a nice break from some of the stresses." He shrugged. "We're not all work."

"I'd love to set something up. My sister-in-law Sophie uses the horses for the riding lessons, so depending on the size of your group, we might have to schedule around her. But if it's three or four people, we have enough that we can make it work any time." Morgan opened a cabinet then paused and craned his neck to peer out the doorway. He reached inside and snagged a clear storage bag of cookies. "Want one?"

"Sure. Are they contraband?"

Morgan managed a sheepish smile as he offered the bag to Dave. "Skye made them for you and your group. I'm not supposed to eat them."

"That's right. You're not." Skye appeared in the doorway tapping her foot. "So I might ask why you are?"

Dave bit into a cookie and his eyebrows lifted. "I imagine it's because they're delicious. You made these?"

Skye blushed prettily. "I did. Thanks. I got the recipe out of the back of a mystery novel I read. The amateur sleuth is a caterer and there are recipes in all the books. These sounded too good to pass up."

"They are. Are those cherries?" Dave picked at what he'd originally thought was a raisin. But it hadn't tasted like any raisin he'd ever encountered.

"Yeah. Pricey, but worth it." Skye eyed the bag.

Dave slid it across the island toward her. "Please have one."

"Are you sure? They're for your group . . ."

"I'm positive. I'm tempted to hoard them for myself instead of sharing with anyone, so this is good for me. Greed isn't an attractive trait in a missionary."

Skye laughed and pulled a cookie out before sealing the bag closed. She pointed a finger at Morgan. "Keep out of those cookies, buster."

"Yes, ma'am."

Dave smiled. Morgan didn't look chastised at all. It was likely that Dave would find him down here snitching another cookie at some point before they all disappeared. He didn't blame Morgan at all. His fingers itched to grab another, so he tucked them in his pockets.

"Are you ready for that tour?" Skye nibbled the edge of her cookie.

Dave popped the last bite of his sandwich into his mouth and carried the plate and glass to the sink.

"There's a dishwasher. Go ahead and load them in. I check it regularly and run it as needed." Skye pointed to the appliance to the left of the sink.

Dave rinsed and loaded the dishes then nodded. "Ready. It was good to meet you, Morgan."

"Thanks. I'm looking forward to seeing what you do with your campers. Let me know about the horseback ride any time."

Skye pointed to the door. "Out. I know you're going to try and get another cookie."

Morgan laughed. He paused to kiss Skye—more than a passing buss of his lips—before striding from the kitchen.

"Still newlyweds?" Dave fought a wistful sigh. People had accused him and Mary of being like newlyweds for all forty-three years they were married.

"Two years at Thanksgiving." She beamed. "It feels like yesterday and forever at the same time."

Dave nodded. "That's exactly right. Congratulations."

"Thanks. Come on through and I'll show you around." Skye led him out of the kitchen, pointing to her office and smaller conference-like rooms as she passed their doors. "Do you think you'll use the guest rooms upstairs?"

"Depends. Is it okay if we roll out sleeping bags on the floor of the main room?" Dave pointed toward the front of the lodge where he'd come in. The big room had some seating areas and tables, but it would still easily accommodate indoor camping for the size group he had.

"I don't see why not." A little line formed between her eyebrows. "It's not going to be comfortable."

He drummed his fingers on his leg. They'd be camping outside for much of the time—would it be bad to let them have relative luxury when they weren't? "Could we take a look at the rooms? Maybe that's the nicer option."

She laughed. "Of course. The stairs are over here."

Dave followed, his gaze roaming over the honey-colored wood. It was a lovely lodge. Rustic, but not overly so. The stairs were tucked away out of sight, but it wasn't a long climb to the guest rooms. The stairs continued up. "There's a third floor?"

"Morgan and I live up there now. It used to be extra rooms, but most of the time our groups use a combination of the cabins and this floor. Or tents. The third floor wasn't getting use, so it made the most sense for us to convert it to our private space."

He nodded. It had been idle curiosity. "It's good that you're right here."

"Oh, you have no idea." She chuckled and unlocked one of the doors that led off the hall. "The rooms share a bathroom between pairs—like Jack and Jill suites."

"May I go in?"

"Please do." Skye stepped back from the door.

Dave wandered in and looked around. It was very much like a college dorm room. Two single beds and two banged-up dressers took up the bulk of the space. There was a desk as well. He pushed on the mattress of one of the beds as he passed it. It was firm, but still better than the floor. The door in the corner led to the bathroom? He twisted the knob and peeked in. No. A closet.

"The bathroom is here." Skye pointed.

He nodded and crossed to the other door and looked in. There was schoolhouse green tile on the walls, a double sink, toilet, and shower stall. Plus a door to what was probably an identical bedroom.

"These are wonderful."

"Thanks. I know they're not like a fancy hotel, but most people who come here aren't looking for that."

Dave chuckled. "No, I don't imagine they are. If it's okay, we'll use these rooms when we aren't out camping. It'll be a nice treat. Maybe the contrast will help them appreciate their luxuries more."

"Great. We don't often have co-ed groups, so I'm not sure what you want to do about that."

"As long as the same genders are in both sides of a suite, I'm not going to worry about it. These are all adults. They know how to behave themselves. And on the flip side, if they don't, they're going to find a way to try and break the rules no matter what I do. Are there any singles? Or non-suites?"

"The corner room on each side." Skye pointed.

"Great. I'd like one of those. Director privilege." He winked. Skye grinned. "And we usually have at least one married couple in each session. It might be nice for them to get a little privacy when we're here."

"That's nice of you. I wondered about that. Thought maybe you'd just split them up anyway."

"Sometimes I do. But this is so nice—and it's an easier introduction—might as well have some mercy."

"Let's head back downstairs and I'll show you where we keep the keys and how to assign and check them out. I have a master," she held it up before relocking the door to the room they'd entered, "so if a key gets lost or locked inside, just come find me, and I'll get it sorted. Do you have my cell programmed into yours?"

"Yes. You have a very thorough set of pre-arrival instructions."

Skye laughed as she started down the stairs. "It feels like every group helps me find something new to add in there. I appreciate your actually reading them. So many don't."

That wasn't surprising. The packet she'd emailed had contained four different PDFs. Each one was at least ten pages. "You run everything here by yourself?"

"I do. If I need help, there are plenty of people at the ranch who can come on the run. Morgan, of course. Then Tommy and Joaquin are usually over here fixing something and I can get either of them to lend a hand in a heartbeat. My sister Indigo would come—she's over at the main ranch and runs a yarn shop, so she's busy, but always makes time when needed. My sister Jade's the same way. My brother Royal, or his wife, Sophie. Even my mom, to be honest, although she always complains that she's too old to be useful." Skye shook her head, frowning slightly.

"Your mother lives on the ranch as well? That's not Betsy?"

"What? Oh, no. Betsy is my grandmother—my dad's mom. My mom, Elise, came here when Dad died. That'll be two years around Thanksgiving, too. I like having her close."

Elise was Skye's mom. And the mother of all the grandchildren Wayne had mentioned in their conversations. How many were there? He tried to think through the names that had come up one way or the other. "There are five siblings? You all live here?"

"Six, actually. My oldest sister, Azure, lives in Virginia with her husband and their daughter."

"Your mother must be remarkable." She'd certainly kept a trim figure. Maybe it was the hiking she did. Or a lucky metabolism. Or both.

"I like to think so." Skye paused by a cabinet hanging beside the big stone fireplace. "The keys are in here."

Dave watched as she opened the door and pointed to the keys hanging neatly on numbered hooks.

"The clipboard here is for signing keys out. Just put the name of anyone in the room and the date the keys are removed. Then when they're returned, date it again. If something gets lost, it's not the end of the world. This system just helps keep keys from walking off."

"Makes sense. How do I know what room is where?" He didn't really want to walk up and down the stairs trying to figure it out and assign keys appropriately.

"Oh. Duh. Sorry." Skye took the clipboard down and flipped it over before handing it to him.

He looked down and let out a relieved breath. There was a map with room numbers. It showed clearly which suites connected. He checked out the corner room across from the stairs before flipping the clipboard back over. "This is great. Thank you. Do you have a pen?"

"Sure." Skye slipped a pen from her pocket and offered it.

Dave wrote down the room number, his name, and the date before looking over the rows of keys and taking the one that should correspond to his room.

"Would you like me to walk you around the main areas outside?"

"I think I'm good. I'll ask if I need something, if that works?"

"Of course."

"Oh. The archery range—is that available for us to use?"

"Sure. The equipment's stored in the little shed there. The key is here." She pointed to a hook labeled "Archery." "If you'd sign it in and out as well, I'd appreciate it. That one seems to walk off more than any of the others."

He nodded. It would. People had to carry it outside and down the road to the range. There were a lot of places to lose it. "I'll try to be careful."

"Do you need anything else? I'm at your disposal to help you get settled, but I also don't want you to feel like you're stuck with me."

Dave laughed. "I wouldn't mind taking my bag up and having a nap. It's been a long day."

"Then I'll let you get to it." Skye hung the clipboard back on its nail before closing the cabinet door. "If you need something, shoot me a text or call. I'm looking forward to having you here."

"Thanks. I'm looking forward to being here. I think God's going to use your camp in extraordinary ways." He smiled, tucked his room key in his pocket, and gave a little wave.

Skye smiled before turning and heading to the stairs.

It was Sunday afternoon—she was probably anxious to spend some relaxing time with her husband. Dave and Mary had always savored their Sunday afternoon rest. He sighed and started toward his car. *Mary, my girl, I wish you were here, but I know you're loving dancing with Jesus. Save me a spot at the Lamb's banquet table.*

He let his mind wander as he grabbed his duffel out of the passenger seat and went back inside.

He shouldn't have been surprised when his thoughts circled back to Elise and their encounter on the mountain.

But he was.

3

Elise bounced her namesake on her knee. The little girl would be one in two more days. Maria was working on food for a party—it would be more low-key than the wedding reception they'd planned last year. But it was fine. Indigo didn't seem to mind sharing the celebration with her daughter—and really, everything had worked out well enough that it would probably continue just fine in the years to come.

"Mom!" The door banged open, and Skye flew in. "Mom? Oh there you are."

"Hi, hon. What's wrong?" She twisted the baby around. "There's Aunt Skye. Say hi."

"Hi hi hi!"

Skye grinned. "Hi, Leecy. Is Indigo here?"

"She's in the back blocking some sweaters. Why?"

"Can she watch the baby while she does that?"

"Of course. It's nearly naptime anyway. What's going on?"

"I have to rush down to Albuquerque. There were six people who missed their flight. Dave thought they'd end up having to make a different camp session, but they were able to squeeze onto another plane. But everyone's busy, so I said I could run down and get them rather than making them deal with a rental car."

"Okay. I'm not sure why you're telling me."

"Can you go hang at the camp and help Dave with the key assignments? I gave him the rundown on Sunday—and he says he's got it—but I just want to make sure it goes as smoothly as possible. He seemed harried."

Elise looked down into the baby's face and tried to squash the nerves in her belly. Dave. She'd been avoiding the camp—and any of the trails that were anywhere near it, just in case—purely because she had no intention of running into him again. But Skye needed her help. Which meant she'd suck it up. Because that was what a mother did. "Let me go tell Indigo and I'll head over. You go ahead and get going—it's a long drive. You're sure you're okay to go alone?"

"Of course. Thanks, Mom." Skye leaned over and kissed her mom's cheek. "I appreciate this. I know it'd probably be fine. But ..."

"But you're a good hostess. It's one of the reasons the camp does so well. Go on. I'll see you when you get back." Elise stood and settled the baby on her hip before heading down the hallway to the bedroom where Indigo was working. Quiet music met her at the doorway. Indigo hummed along as she smoothed knitted material on a board and pushed pins into it.

"Mama! Ma-ma-ma-ma!" The baby wiggled out of Elise's arms and toddled across the floor before wrapping her chubby arms around Indigo's leg.

"Hi, baby." Indigo glanced down, then looked over her shoulder. "Hey, Mom."

"Hi. Skye needs me over at the camp. Is that okay?"

"Of course. I've got the munchkin. It's nearly time for her morning nap anyway."

"You're sure?" Not that there was really another option. Elise had told Skye to go. Had said she'd go over to the camp, so why was she hoping against hope for a reprieve?

"Don't be silly, Mom. Of course I am. Go help Skye. I'll see you tomorrow."

Elise managed a tight smile. Great. Time around Dave wasn't anything she needed. She didn't need to have the kinds of feelings he'd awakened on their short hike down the mountain. Those sorts of feelings had no point at her age. She'd had her love—maybe it wasn't a great love, the kind that books and movies would be made about—but it had been comfortable.

She headed out of the fiber cabin and onto the trail that would lead her to the camp. It was warm, but not hot. Typical for August in the mountains of New Mexico. Her first year here, she'd been surprised. She'd always imagined New Mexico was hot year round. Albuquerque got hot in the summer, and Betsy and Wayne said the southern part of the state was what people expected. Elise hadn't gone on any of the sightseeing trips around the state that her kids had taken. They'd invited her, but she didn't want to be a third wheel. Her kids were married now—it was good to let them live their lives.

People milled around in front of the lodge. There were piles of backpacks and other luggage as well spread out in the parking area. Where was Dave?

She scanned the crowd, but all the people she saw were young. Almost impossibly young to her eyes. They were going to be missionaries? They looked like babies.

Elise climbed the stairs and entered the lodge. It was less chaotic inside, but not by much. Just how many people did he have coming to this camp?

"Oh, thank goodness, you're here." Sighing, Dave grabbed her arm. "I thought I had it under control when Skye left, and then it all went sideways."

Despite herself, Elise laughed. "It's not that bad. What are you trying to do?"

"I need to get rooms assigned and let everyone take their baggage up—get settled."

Elise looked around the room and considered the crowd outside. "What's your plan?"

"Honestly? My plan was for Margaret to handle this."

"Who's Margaret?" She wasn't jealous. That would be ridiculous—she didn't even know who this woman was. Or, for that matter, who Dave was. Not in any way that mattered.

"She's from the agency. She and her husband were supposed to be here so she could serve as a mentor and confidant of sorts to the girls."

"Oh. Did they miss the plane? They're part of that group?"

"If only." Dave shook his head. "She fell this morning on the way to the airport and broke her leg. They're not coming at all."

"Oh my." Elise pressed her lips together to keep from chuckling. It wasn't a laughing matter. "How can I help?"

"You had six kids. Maybe you know how to get a group to gather up, sit down, and listen?"

"Only five. But sure." Elise considered a moment before walking to the door and leaning out. She placed two fingers in her mouth and gave a piercing whistle. The chatter settled. When it was quiet enough, she cleared her throat. "Can you all come inside and grab a seat? We'll get rooms assigned and go over the plan for today."

Dave stared at her.

"What?"

"That was impressive."

Heat crawled across her cheeks. "Yes, well. Five kids. They could get rowdy. It paid to learn how to get attention fast."

"I was sure Skye said six."

She probably had. Jade definitely counted as part of the

family, but Elise hadn't done anything to birth or raise her. As much as Elise had come to love Jade, she wasn't one of the kids that got counted when Elise added them up. But it was a lot to get into right now, and not worth it. She nodded toward the gathered and seated group. "Let's get going while we have their attention."

"Right. Of course. Do you know where the keys are?"

"Sure. I'll get the clipboard while you explain what's happening. You have a list of your campers, right?"

"A list?"

"How were you planning to split them up?"

"Oh. Um. Margaret." He sighed. "I have all the names on my phone."

"We'll wing it. Go say hello and at least introduce yourself. Maybe check that Margaret hasn't emailed you something that would help?"

"That's a good idea." He slipped his phone out of his pocket and scrolled. "She did. You're both lifesavers."

Elise shook her head. He was like a distracted little boy. "Good. Now go get started."

"Right." He flashed a grin before he strode over to the front of the group and clasped his hands behind his back. "Okay, everyone, listen up. I'm Dave Fitzgerald. Thanks for coming. Let's start everything off with prayer."

She watched as everyone obediently bowed their heads and folded their hands in their laps. Was it comforting to have found faith so young? When she'd been their age—or at least the age she imagined they were—she'd been a young mother. So in love with Martin that the idea of following him around from job to job and scraping by in whatever accommodations he drummed up for them had seemed like an adventure. Honestly, after the first years, living on the converted school bus was almost a luxury.

Elise moved to the cabinet by the fireplace and opened it to grab the clipboard. She carried it back with her as she scooted closer to the group.

Dave had finished praying and was giving a brief overview of their plans. "For today, we're going to take it easy. There are nice rooms here at the lodge. You'll have a roommate, and shared bathrooms, but don't get too used to it. We're only staying in the guest rooms for two nights at the front of our experience. We'll be back again toward the end."

There were groans from some of the seated clusters, and Elise hid a smile. She agreed with that sentiment completely. She was getting too old to camp.

"This is Elise Hewitt. She's going to be handing out keys. I'll call out names in pairs—you'll be roommates. When I call your name, I'll give you a room number. You'll tell Elise that number, she'll sign out a key. Then you'll take your gear up and get settled. We have three hours before supper, and that time's your own. If you're someone who can nap without it impacting your ability to sleep at night, I recommend it." Dave pulled out his phone and scrolled. "Okay, let's start with Gabriella and Jane. Room two."

Two women—one willowy thin, the other just this side of obese—stood and started picking their way across the room toward Elise.

Elise copied down their names and dated the form, then pointed out the stairs. By the time the girls were done, two men were waiting. One was swallowing nervously. Hopefully he'd get over that, or he was going to annoy everyone with his constantly bobbing Adam's apple.

It took about a half an hour to work through the whole group. When all the keys had been distributed, Elise hung the clipboard on its nail and shut the nearly empty cabinet.

Dave, hands tucked in his pockets, wandered her way. "Thank you. I don't think I could have done that without you."

"Oh, I'm sure you'd have figured it out. You were a missionary for how many years?"

"Almost forty. But I had Mary to keep me on my toes." His smile was wistful. "She was definitely the organized one of the two of us. She used to joke that her spiritual gift of administration was the pinky toe of the gifts—not glamorous, but you notice when it's missing."

Elise chuckled. Spiritual gifts were still a strange concept. She'd been reading more about them lately—part of trying to settle the general restlessness that saturated her. Maybe if she knew what God was asking her to do with the rest of her life she'd be satisfied. Settled. There had to be more than babysitting into her golden years. "I'm happy to have been able to help. Can I do anything else?"

"I think we're set. Again, I appreciate it. Would you like to join us for dinner? It's nothing fancy. Sloppy joes, I believe, with coleslaw and a salad. But there's bound to be more than enough."

"With sloppy joes there usually is." Elise pressed her lips together and considered. It wasn't as though she had a thousand options. She could join Betsy and Wayne at the main house—Maria always made plenty so that whoever wanted to could drop in and get a hot meal. She could throw something together in her own cabin. That was her usual choice. Elise didn't want to be a burden—to her in-laws or to her kids—and they'd all made it clear she was welcome anytime as well. Now there was the possibility of sloppy joes with a lodgeful of strangers. And Dave. The fact that he entered into consideration should be the reason she said no. "You're sure it's okay?"

His eyes brightened. "Let's go track down the cook and

double-check, if you're worried. But I've never known there not to be room for one more."

Before she could object, Dave was walking toward the kitchen. Elise huffed out a little breath and started after him.

"I feel like I'm imposing."

"Nonsense. I'm serious." He smiled at her over his shoulder before rapping smartly on the kitchen doorframe. "Jillian, right?"

"That's right, Mr. Fitzgerald."

Elise peered in and some of her nerves eased. Jillian was one of the college kids at church. She was a sweetheart. "Hi, Jillian."

"Hi, Mrs. Hewitt. How are you?"

"I'm doing well. I didn't realize you were doing the cooking for the camp. Don't you have to go back to school later this month?"

Jillian's smile faltered a little before she shored it up. "Oh. Well, no. I'm going to take a semester off and save some money."

Poor thing. This was supposed to be her final year. "Do you have another job arranged for after the camps end?"

"Not yet, but I know God will come through. He always does." Jillian looked back at Dave. "Did you need me to do something, Mr. Fitzgerald?"

"I was actually wondering if you thought there'd be enough dinner for Elise to join us."

"Oh, sure. I planned for extra—I know how guys eat. My brother's only sixteen but some days he eats like he's four people. I didn't want anyone to be left hungry."

"That's settled then." Dave turned his mesmerizing gaze on Elise. "You'll join us?"

"I . . . yes. Thank you." She looked away as her cheeks heated. What was wrong with her? She wasn't a teenager. "I'm looking forward to the meal now that I know Jillian's in charge. She's an incredible cook."

The girl turned beet red. "Thanks, Mrs. Hewitt. Five o'clock is still when you want me to set up the serving line, right?"

"That'll be great. Let me know if you need some strong backs and able hands to help you with that. I'll send some of the gang."

"Thanks, Mr. Fitzgerald. I won't say no."

"All right. I'll have some check in around five. Thanks, Jillian."

What was she thinking? Elise turned and wandered back toward the main lounge. She should have said no. She'd meant to say no.

"Where do you know Jillian from?"

Elise started. The man was like a ninja.

"Sorry." He laid a hand on her arm with a quiet chuckle.

"It's fine. It's not like I didn't know you were here." Elise took a deep breath and let it out slowly. Something had to work to slow her heartbeat. "Um. Jillian goes to our church. She's frequently in charge of the refreshments in the foyer when she's home on break. I believe she's active with the homeless and shut-in meals as well."

"Any idea why she's taking a semester off?"

"Just speculation. And most of that's based on gossip."

Dave nodded. "I wouldn't want you to feel like I'm pushing you to speak out of turn."

"I don't know. It's common knowledge at church." She bit her lip. Dave didn't go to their church, though. And Jillian deserved to have a place—even if it was only for a couple of months—where she didn't have to deal with the pitying side-eyes. "I guess, generally, it's not wrong to say she comes from a hard situation at home."

"So what money she should be spending on tuition is likely going to help out?"

Elise lifted a shoulder. That was possible. It was more likely that her father had poured it down his throat. Everyone knew the man had been on a big bender in June—one that had landed him in jail and then rehab. Jail, at least, didn't cost money. Jillian's mother kept insisting that her husband just needed help, so she kept throwing more money into treatment that never seemed to stick.

"Hmm. I make it a point to pray for all the people involved in our camps, so I already put Jillian on the list, but I'll add her family, too."

"That's nice of you."

"What about you, Elise?"

"What about me?"

"How can I pray for you?"

She blinked and had to stop herself from taking a step back. "I don't—why would you—I'm not part of your crew."

"I don't *only* pray for the camp family."

She nodded. Of course not. "I'm fine. But thank you for the thought."

His eyebrows lifted but he didn't speak for several heartbeats. Then he nodded. "All right. Well, God knows what you need. So I'll just ask Him to take care of it for you."

"Okay." Elise swallowed. "I should probably go back to my daughter's yarn shop for a bit in case she needs me. But I can be back at five for supper."

"Okay." Dave tucked his hands in his pockets. "I'll look forward to seeing you then. Thanks again for your help this afternoon."

"Sure. No problem. I'll see you later." Elise waved—like an idiot, who did that?—and hurried toward the door. She wasn't quite running.

But boy did she want to.

Dave Fitzgerald wasn't the kind of man she was used to dealing with. Not in any way. How did he switch from absent-minded professor who couldn't figure out how to call a group to order to someone who was not only praying for a girl he barely knew, but for Elise?

For that matter, what kind of person was so casual about the fact that they were going to pray for someone? It sounded like he meant it, too. It wasn't the "Oh, I'll pray for you" lip service that seemed to be like breathing to most of the Christians she'd encountered at church and around town. Not that some of them didn't mean it. Just not most of them.

Dave clearly meant it.

And something about the way he said it suggested he had more insight into her being than he should on short acquaintance. That made him dangerous.

Elise Hewitt wasn't a woman looking for danger.

4

D ave's smile faded as Elise practically sprinted out of the lodge. His shoulders fell. That had gone badly. Should he not have invited her to dinner? It seemed like the least he could do to thank her for helping out. No matter how it looked, he'd been at sea and sinking fast—Margaret's text letting him know she wasn't coming at all had shaken him. He counted on Margaret—and Herb, her husband—to make these camps work. They were never meant to be a one-man show.

He dug his phone out of his pocket and scrolled to Margaret's contact. He'd check in—maybe he could convince her to come later.

"Hi, Dave. Looks like Herb owes me twenty." Margaret's laugh was as round and full as ever.

"Thanks a lot, Dave." Herb shouted in the background.

Dave shook his head and wandered over to one of the couches in the lounge area. "I'm stunned, frankly, that two dedicated missionaries would be betting on anything."

"Is it betting if it's a sure thing?" Margaret's voice held warmth and mirth. "How's it going?"

"I got the room keys assigned. Everyone's upstairs settling in.

I gave them free time until dinner. I figure that's soon enough to start the program."

"Seems reasonable." She paused and Dave could practically hear her thinking. "What's wrong?"

"Wrong? Nothing. What could be wrong? I'm here with twenty bright-eyed missionary wannabes with no help. Are you sure you can't come? Maybe next week when you're more secure on your crutches?" He hated that he could hear a hint of whining in his own voice, but he needed them.

"Sorry, no. They said I might need surgery. The doctor wants to look at it again next week when the swelling is down, and reevaluate."

Dave winced. That was more serious than he'd imagined. "Oh."

"Yeah. I'm really sorry, Dave. On the flip side, I know you're going to be fine. I don't usually go out in the field with you—once you get out there, you're on your own anyway."

"Other than knowing that the women can come back and check in with you—debrief a little, or just blow off steam—when things get to be too much. You can't tell me that doesn't happen the whole time."

She paused. "No, you're right. It does. Couldn't you ask Betsy Hewitt to fill in? Seems to me she'd be willing to make herself available."

"I forgot you know the Hewitts."

"'Knew' might be more accurate. It's been years since we had any contact."

"Be that as it may, that's why we're here—you mentioned the ranch, I looked it up and made a call." Dave sighed and ran a hand through his hair. "You really think Betsy would do it?"

"I think it's worth asking her."

"Yeah, okay. I'll be praying for your leg to not need surgery. Are you in pain?"

"It's managed. So far at least."

"Okay. I'll pray for that, too. And for Herb."

"Herb doesn't need prayer."

"Sure he does. He's taking care of you, right?"

Margaret laughed. "I'm not a bad patient, am I, hon?"

"Yes, dear. I mean, no, dear." Herb chuckled in the background.

"Hm. Maybe he does need prayer after all. I might just kill him if he keeps that up."

Dave smiled at the easy teasing between his friends. He'd had that once, with Mary. He missed it more than he realized. "I'll let you go. Feel better."

"I'm sure I will eventually. I'm really sorry."

"Hey, accidents happen. I won't hold it against you too much. Just ten, maybe fifteen years."

"You're as bad as Herb. Go talk to Betsy. And tell her hi from us."

"Will do. Bye." He ended the call and let his head drop back. He closed his eyes and spent a few minutes praying for Margaret and Herb. And Elise. He couldn't keep her out of his mind, so he might as well pray for her, too.

"Mr. Fitzgerald?"

He opened his eyes. "Hi, Jillian."

"I was thinking I could set out a little snack in case anyone was munchie before dinner. Is that all right?"

"It's a great idea. Thank you."

She smiled, her cheeks pinking. "I just wanted to be sure it was okay."

"Food is always okay." Had he ever been that young? She seemed particularly innocent. Was it because of her home life? He'd wanted to pry for details, but it also didn't seem wise to encourage gossip when it was clear Elise was working to avoid that.

"All right. I'll try to mix healthy options in with sweet."

"Thanks." He watched her start back toward the kitchen. "Oh, Jillian?"

She turned, eyebrows raised.

"Do you know the best way over to the main part of the ranch? I could drive around, but there has to be a trail, doesn't there?"

"Oh, sure. You can't miss it. If you go left when you leave out the front, you'll see it."

"Appreciate it." Dave pushed to his feet. "If anyone asks, I'll be back in time for dinner."

"Okay. Enjoy your walk—it's a nice day for it."

Dave wandered out the front door and drew in a deep breath. Jillian was right. It was a beautiful day. To the left and he couldn't miss it. He shook his head. He wasn't too sure about that—but maybe it was the same trail he'd found wandering back from his hike on Sunday afternoon.

He started that direction, then glanced left again. And there was the path. How had he missed it before? He turned and continued down the short side of the lodge and toward the smudge of buildings he could see in the distance. How far was it? Maybe he would've been better off driving, though a walk would do him good.

Elise had come on foot.

That didn't mean it was close. She looked fit. And he had no business thinking about her figure. It felt disloyal to Mary, if nothing else. His wife had always been comfortably plump—even when they'd lived where regular meals weren't a guarantee and lots of effort was expended on a daily basis. Something about her genetics had always made her hold on to the weight. It had driven her crazy, though he'd never minded.

Not that Mary had believed that.

Dave blew out a breath and pushed the thoughts away. He

was past this. He and Mary had so many wonderful years together. He savored them. He was grateful to Jesus for them. And now? He could be glad his love lived beyond the pain and sickness that had haunted her last days. Now Mary worshipped at Jesus' feet—exactly the place she'd longed to be. He'd see her again.

He slowed his steps as he reached a row of cabins. He frowned. This didn't look like the area where he and Elise had come out from the trail on Sunday. He stopped, shaded his eyes, and slowly turned. No—the mountain was definitely over there. So there were more cabins here. One of them was probably the yarn shop, if he'd understood the various bits and pieces he'd overheard. He could investigate. But he didn't want Elise to think he was following her. Plus, he needed to find Betsy and nail down a mentor for the ladies.

What was he going to do if she said no?

He sent up a quick prayer. There really needed to be someone for the women to talk to—he was happy to listen, but there were always things they weren't comfortable talking to an older man about. He didn't blame them.

"Hey there, Dave. What brings you out this way?"

Dave paused and glanced over, smiling when his gaze landed on Morgan. The younger man tossed a bale of hay onto a pile and dusted off his hands. "I'm looking for Betsy Hewitt, actually."

Morgan's eyebrows lifted. "She's probably up at the main house. Want me to call over and double-check? Sometimes she goes to hang out at the fiber cabin with Elise and Indigo."

"Is it a problem if I just wander up and check?"

"No. Course not. If no one answers when you knock, come back here and we can call—save you running around the ranch looking for her. I'll be around the stables."

"Thanks." Dave watched as Morgan disappeared into the

stable. The horses greeted him, and Morgan's quiet murmur barely reached his ears. Shaking his head, Dave continued down the path toward the main house, taking note of the riding rings and general layout of the working part of the ranch. It was a nice looking operation.

There was a door on the back of the house, but that was probably for family. Better to continue on around to the front and ring the doorbell. Would they have one? Surely they had some mechanism for unexpected visitors.

Dave studied the stucco house. It stood out from the rest of the buildings—at least the ones he'd seen. But it still fit in. It was, if nothing else, very New Mexico. He spotted the doorbell and pressed it.

After a minute, the door opened and an older man answered. "Can I help you?"

"Are you Wayne Hewitt? I'm Dave Fitzgerald."

"Dave!" Wayne's face split into a grin. "It's good to meet you in person. Come in, come in. Can I get you something to drink? Or a snack? Maria made some cookies the other day. They're amazing."

"I wouldn't say no to a cookie. Maybe some water?" Dave smiled and followed Wayne deeper into the house. "I'm sorry to just drop by."

"Nonsense. I was hoping you'd be able to. I've enjoyed our phone calls and have been looking forward to getting to say hello face-to-face." Wayne pointed to a row of chairs tucked up under a long counter. "Grab yourself a seat and I'll get the snack. You sure you want water? We have some soda hiding in the fridge."

"That's fine, too. Whatever's easy." Dave wasn't usually a big soda drinker, but he didn't have anything against it. "Is your wife around? I actually had a question I was hoping to ask her."

"Betsy?" Wayne's eyebrows lifted, but he nodded. "Sure.

She's in the office. Let me set out a snack for her, too, and I'll go get her."

"Thanks." Dave reached for the can of soda and popped the top.

"Tuck in. I'll be right back."

Dave eyed the plate of cookies. They were large—the size of his palm—and the chunks of chocolate and nuts were visible bumps on the top. They probably weren't going to be as good as the cookies Skye had stocked in the lodge kitchen. But then, he'd never had another cookie that was. He picked up one of the discs and took a bite.

Well, okay, they were close.

He closed his eyes and chewed.

"Maria has a gift."

Dave's cheeks heated and he turned to look at the woman who was in the process of sliding onto the stool beside him. "She does. She's your cook?"

"Among other things—including granddaughter-in-law. I'm Betsy."

"Dave Fitzgerald. Nice to meet you." He brushed the crumbs off his hand before offering it.

"Wayne said you wanted to see me?" Betsy took a cookie and opened her soda.

"You say that like you don't trust me to have gotten the message right." Wayne shook his head and reached across for a cookie.

"Well, you never know." Betsy chuckled. "So what can I do for you?"

It was a good opening. "Usually my friends and coworkers, Margaret and Herb, are part of the camp staff."

"Sure. Wayne mentioned that. We know them, slightly—or used to. When we were all younger. They worked on the reservation for a number of years and our church is active with those ministries and outreaches as well."

"Ah. Margaret said to say hello." He hadn't known that his friends had gone to the Native Americans. How had that never come up in any conversation over the years?

"I hope she'll come down and catch up when you have a little breather." Betsy nibbled the edge of her cookie.

"That's just it. They aren't coming. Margaret tripped over their cat when they were getting ready to head to the airport. She broke her leg and may end up needing surgery."

"Oh my. I'll add her to the prayer list at church and my own as well. But I guess I'm still not sure how I'm supposed to help."

"One of the big things Margaret did was mentor the women. It's mostly being available to talk to—sometimes it gets hard and you just need to be able to vent or cry or get prayer. I do that for the men, but since it's one on one and we try to keep it private, behind closed doors, it doesn't seem like a good idea for the genders to be mixed."

Betsy nodded slowly. "That makes sense."

"Do you think you'd be willing? Do you have the time? I can send the ladies down to the house here, if that helps make it easier for you."

Betsy and Wayne exchanged a rueful look.

Wayne cleared his throat. "Normally, I can tell you Betsy would jump up and dance at an opportunity like that."

"But?" Dave could feel the hope leaking out of him like a balloon with a hole in it.

"I'm flying out tomorrow to go see our other granddaughter and her husband and baby. Azure and Matt had originally planned to come here this summer. They've been wanting to spend more time with Elise and everyone, but Matt's a mechanic and he owns his own garage and I guess their plans for someone to run the shop while they were out of town fell through. So I'm going to go to them."

Dave nodded. "And Elise will go, too, I imagine?"

"She would if she wasn't so stubborn." Betsy frowned at her cookie before taking a bite.

"I don't understand." Dave reached for his soda.

"Elise doesn't have the money for a ticket, and she wouldn't let us pay for it." Wayne sighed. "It was one of those things that we finally agreed we shouldn't push anymore. I'm not sure Azure agrees, but maybe we'll be able to get her to come back with Betsy for a bit."

There shouldn't be a little thread of relief winding through his heart. He barely knew Elise. Why would it matter that she was staying at the ranch? Except, of course, that he'd like to get to know her. And even that wasn't wise—that wasn't why he was here. He needed to stay focused on the camp and on the future missionaries he was training. God's mission was more important than any curiosity he might feel about a woman.

"Actually, that's an idea." Betsy tapped her finger on the side of the soda can.

"What is?" Dave looked over. Why was Betsy smiling like that?

"Why don't you ask Elise? She raised three daughters. I'm guessing she knows a little something about mentoring young women."

"Do you think she'd do it?" His heart had started to race. It would be nice to have an excuse to spend more time with her. To get to know her better. As a friend, of course. That was all.

Wayne laughed. "Only one way to find out. Why don't you go ask her? She's at the fiber cabin with Indigo."

"I can wait. She's going to join us at the camp for supper."

"She is?" If he'd said Elise was going to tap dance on top of a horse, he didn't think Betsy could have looked more surprised.

Dave nodded.

"Well. Good for you, if she shows up. Ask her. Remind her I'm going to be out of town if she balks."

He studied Betsy a moment. "You think she will?"

"Oh, I'm fairly positive. But maybe your asking will get her to reconsider coming with me to see Azure." Betsy grinned. "I'll win either way. Of course, if she does that you'll be out of luck. Hmm."

"Maybe Maria could, if Elise won't." Wayne rested his elbows on the table. "She's not older, so you'd lose some of that mentor feeling, but she's got a strong faith."

Betsy nodded. "Or we can think up some of the ladies at church to ask. I still think Elise is the best first stop, though."

Dave took a deep breath and tried to juggle the options in his mind. He didn't know anyone he could get to come out at such short notice. He'd like to spend more time with Elise—or at least to have an excuse to get to know her better. Maybe he shouldn't, but it didn't change what he felt. So he'd ask her and pray that God would steer her heart the way He wanted it to go. "I'll talk to Elise. Maybe start working on that list though, just in case. At the end of the day, the ladies in the camp need someone available. That's the bottom line."

"I'll start on it now. But I'll be praying Elise says yes. I think it'd be good for her to have something to do. And don't let her tell you she hasn't been a believer long enough."

Dave slid off the stool and nodded, even though he wanted to sigh. Just how many objections was he going to have to overcome at once? Was it likely Elise wouldn't come to dinner like she'd agreed? Maybe he should find her now, just in case. "She's at the yarn shop?"

"Should be." Wayne gestured vaguely in the direction that Dave had come from. "You can't miss it if you stay on the path. Look for yarn in the front windows."

"Okay. Thanks." Dave started toward the front door. He'd walk slowly—more time to think and pray about his approach. No matter how much *he* wanted Elise to take this on, it needed to be what God wanted first.

He'd learned a long time ago that nothing good ever came from pushing his will in front of God's.

5

Elise eyed the spinning wheel dubiously. "I don't think this is a good idea."

"Mom." Frustration leaked through Indigo's tone. "You're ready. You've been ready for six months. Or more. If you don't want to learn to spin, that's one thing, but if you do, the only way you learn is to sit down and try."

"What if I mess it up?" She glanced down at the roving in the basket at her feet. It was dyed a lovely emerald green and was softer than anything she'd spun on the drop spindle yet. It was important. Not something that should be handed to a beginner to learn on. "Maybe you have something that's not so pretty for me to work with?"

Indigo shook her head. "We've been over this. I custom dyed this. The order fell through. Right now? That roving isn't worth anything to me. If we can get it spun so we can list and sell it, maybe we can recoup some of the investment."

"I just don't see why—"

Indigo's sigh ended on an exasperated grunt. "Just get started, Mom. You know what to do. If it's awful and you ruin it, then I'll let you pay me what I would have charged for the roving, okay?"

Elise hunched her shoulders but nodded. That, at least, was something. Yes, she wanted to learn. And yes, doing was the best way to learn. But Indigo had already given Elise so much, she was hesitant to take more. She *hated* depending on the kindness and generosity of her children and in-laws. But there were no other options unless she left the ranch and moved . . . somewhere . . . and got a regular job. And that wasn't something she was qualified to do. It had been decades since she'd been a part of the workforce. Nobody wanted to hire an unqualified fifty-three-year-old to do anything.

She could almost feel Indigo's gaze as she gave the spinning wheel a little push before picking up the rhythm with the foot pedals. Elise tugged on the roving and fed it onto the spindle.

"That looks good. Keep going, Mom. You're doing great." Indigo patted Elise's shoulder then moved off.

Elise fought the panic that began to well in her chest. Why wasn't her daughter going to stay and watch? What if—no. No what-ifs. Indigo was right. Elise could do this. And if she couldn't, then she couldn't, and she'd buy the finished yarn and make another lumpy scarf out of it. Or maybe she'd try her hand at a cowl. Her knitting was improving. She was probably ready for a more challenging pattern.

There was a rap at the door before it swung open, setting the jingle bells on top into their cheerful cacophony of welcome.

Elise glanced over and her feet faltered on the spinning wheel pedals. She dragged her attention back to the yarn and managed to stop spinning without creating a mess on the spool. "Hi, Dave. Um. Are you lost?"

He chuckled and shut the door behind him. "You'd think so, wouldn't you? I was looking for you, actually."

"Oh?" He was probably coming to let her know they didn't

have enough for her at dinner after all. And that was fine. She had food at her cabin. Maybe she'd been looking forward to seeing all those eager, young faces again—to soaking up their energy and excitement—but not joining them was better. It wasn't as if she'd ever fit in with the missionary crowd. Not with the life she'd lived. "Why?"

He cleared his throat and glanced around the cabin. "This is a nice-looking operation you've got here."

"It's not mine. It belongs to my daughter Indigo. Would you like a tour?"

"Actually, yes. I'm always interested in learning new things." He nodded at the spinning wheel. "I don't think I've ever seen one of those in person. I didn't think modern cultures even used them anymore."

Elise laughed. "I would have said the same thing a handful of years ago. Indigo's doing well by it, though."

"And you, looks like."

Elise turned away and studied the yarn on the spool. It wasn't much, but it didn't look terrible. If she was honest, it actually looked fine. Huh. "I'm still learning." But she stood and set the roving aside.

"So this is the storefront?"

"That's kind of grand, but sure. We don't get a lot of in-person traffic. It's a haul up to the ranch from town. Most of our sales are online. But we also have a consignment agreement with one of the craft galleries in town. That's been a good expansion—and it's started bringing some foot traffic our way when the shop doesn't have the colors or blends that someone's looking for." Elise shrugged. "Indigo does a lot of the spinning in here, too."

Dave reached out, then pulled his hand back. "Is it okay to touch?"

"Sure." Most people didn't even think to ask. Then again,

most of the people who came here knew yarn—and so they knew that touching was the only real way to get a feel for the product. She watched as he stroked several of the skeins hanging on the wall. "Over here's the drying room. Indigo dyes the wool—sometimes before it's spun, sometimes after. I'm not clear on which is better or why she changes it up."

"You haven't asked." Indigo poked her head out from behind one of the floor-to-ceiling drying racks and grinned. "I'm Indigo. You're the missionary man?"

"That's me. Generally I go by Dave, though. It's shorter."

Elise laughed.

Indigo chuckled. "Nice to meet you. Are you really here to learn about yarn?"

"No. But I don't figure it's ever wrong to learn something new. I wanted to talk to your mom about something."

Indigo gave him a long, measuring look.

Elise shook her head. She recognized that glint in her daughter's eye and there was no point in letting her get her hopes up. There was no potential for romance here—and why did her daughters keep thinking that was what Elise needed, anyway? "I imagine you're going to rescind the dinner invite. And that's fine. I definitely don't want to take food away from someone who's going to need it. I appreciate that you thought to invite me."

Dave turned, frowning. "What? No, that's not it at all."

"Mom." Indigo's mutter held censure.

"Oh. Well, it's still perfectly fine. I don't want to intrude." Elise wanted to hunch her shoulders, but forced them to relax. Maybe she'd put him on the spot so he felt he had to lie. Did missionaries lie? Maybe not.

"You're not intruding." Dave cocked his head to the side. "Didn't we talk to Jillian and confirm there was more than plenty?"

"Well, yes." Now she did hunch her shoulders.

"So we'll see you at five." He paused, cleared his throat. "I was, in fact, going to see if you might be available to help out a little for this first camp session, at a minimum."

"Help out? You don't have to check the keys in and out every day." What else could she possibly help with? She didn't know anything about being a missionary. And she certainly had no intention of getting close to the obstacle course that Tommy and Joaquin had built for these camps. Rope climbing, crossing boards twenty feet above the ground, and then climbing a big A-frame with slats up one side and a cargo net on the other? No, thank you. "I don't see how I could."

"Why don't you let him talk, Mom? He'd probably explain what he had in mind."

Elise shot her daughter a quelling look.

Indigo held up her hands and scooted toward the door. "I'll be down in the blocking room if you need me."

"She's not wrong." Dave sounded more amused than anything. "Maybe we could go sit on the couch in the main room and I could explain before you shoot me down?"

"I wasn't trying to—" Elise cut herself off and closed her eyes. She took a deep breath before forcing a smile and gesturing to the door. "Of course. I'm sorry."

"After you." Dave waited for Elise to slip through the door ahead of him.

She didn't like knowing he was walking behind her. It made her too aware of him. Like when they'd been on the trail, on the mountain, and he'd been this presence behind her. Watching her. Making her wonder just what, exactly, he saw.

She sat and folded her hands in her lap before shooting him an expectant look.

Dave took the cushion farthest away from her. There was

certainly nothing inappropriate about it. And there was no reason for her to be nervous.

"I mentioned Margaret and Herb."

"The organized woman who keeps you on track."

He laughed. "That's Margaret. Turns out she broke her leg and may need surgery."

"So she won't be coming at all." Elise frowned. "I still don't see how I can help. I'm not a missionary. Never have been."

"I get that. But you're a woman. You've raised children. You love Jesus. Other than helping me stay organized, Margaret has always stood in as a sounding board for the women in the group. Someone to talk to when things are hard, or they just need a listening ear. Betsy said she thought you might be just the one for the job."

"Betsy said?" Had the woman lost her mind? Elise shook her head. "That's insane."

"I don't think it is."

"You're just desperate, that's all." She held up a hand when he started to speak again. "No, look. You're right. I am a woman and have raised five kids. And I do love Jesus. But you're missing the part where that's new. I didn't grow up in church. I haven't spent most of my life trying to follow Him. When I was the age of the people at your camp I was living with Martin Hewitt and raising our first two babies without the benefit of marriage. We never did get married. And I never regretted that fact until recently."

She watched as Dave jolted, clearly taken aback. It put a little crack in her heart, but that was fine. He needed to understand that she wasn't some paragon of virtue who could help young women understand anything about living for Jesus. She barely understood it herself.

"Skye said she had five siblings. Six total."

Of course that was what he latched on to. Elise sighed. "Jade. Have you met Jade?"

He shook his head.

"She's Martin's daughter. We found out about her a couple of years ago now—just before Martin passed." Elise watched to be sure he understood, then nodded. "Exactly. So you see, I'm not the woman you're looking for. You're better off going back to Betsy and getting her to do it for you."

"She's leaving tomorrow."

Right. Betsy was heading to Virginia to visit Azure and Matt. And the grandbaby she hadn't met in person yet. Just over video call. Elise wanted to go more than she wanted to breathe her next breath, but she wasn't going to be beholden to Wayne and Betsy any more than she already was. Oh, she probably had the money to pay for the ticket. The kids had all given her what they'd inherited from Martin, but that was all socked away. It was the only money she had, unless she could figure out some sort of income in the meantime. She couldn't fritter it away on plane tickets every time the whim struck. "There has to be someone else who can do it."

Dave held her gaze before slowly nodding. "There probably is. Does it change anything if I tell you I'm not interested in finding someone else to do it?"

"Why?" The man made no sense. "I'm completely unqualified for this. Why would you want to set me up to fail? Why would you want to set your campers up to fail?"

A corner of his mouth poked up and the hint of a dimple appeared in his cheek. "I don't believe that's what's happening here at all. I think this is something God wants for you, and for the campers."

Elise shook her head. Missionary work had always seemed a little on the crazy side. This was just driving that home.

"Tell you what. It's another . . ." he glanced at the watch on his wrist, ". . . hour and a half until dinner. Pray about it between now and then. If you get a clear signal from God that this isn't for you, let me know then. I'll be praying for the same thing. But if you don't? Will you at least give it a try?"

Elise shrunk back. She didn't know the first thing about praying for clear signals. She prayed—or tried to—usually focusing on being thankful for the blessings she saw in her life. She didn't ask God for things. She certainly didn't ask for direction. This was where she was. Elise figured God had put her here so she might as well be grateful for it. "I . . ." Something in his gaze choked off her objection. "I guess I can try."

"Great." Dave reached over and lightly patted her arm before standing. "Then I'll look forward to seeing you at dinner and introducing you, officially, to the crew."

"You're confident, aren't you?"

He just grinned.

Elise sighed. "Five?"

"Five o'clock."

She nodded and watched as he left the cabin. When the door closed behind him, Elise sagged back and closed her eyes. This was insane. God couldn't possibly want her to volunteer to mentor women who knew more about loving Jesus than she probably ever would. Could He?

"I think you should do it." Indigo flopped onto the couch beside Elise and patted her knee. The baby started to fuss from the back bedroom where she napped and Indigo turned with a laugh. She pushed back up to her feet. "I'm going to go get her, but I think you need to say yes."

"Do you know how to pray for direction?" Elise frowned at her daughter. She was even younger to the faith than Elise— okay, only by a few weeks, and yet.

Indigo jerked a shoulder. "I guess just like any prayer. You talk to God. He's not fussy about language. You know that."

"Yeah. All right. You think I can keep spinning while I pray?"

Indigo leaned over and kissed Elise's head. "I do it all the time."

Elise smiled and watched Indigo move down the hall. Somewhere along the line all her children had turned into solid, mature adults. She wasn't sure she'd had as much to do with it as she'd always thought she would. Most of it was probably the grace of God.

She blew out a breath and moved to the spinning wheel. As she got back into the rhythm of feeding fiber to the machine, a thought flitted through her brain. *God doesn't call the prepared. He prepares the called.*

6

Dave glanced at his watch again. She was only five minutes late. Mary had consistently been behind schedule by at least twice that. For all that his wife had been an organizing genius, she'd been late to everything. And it was better to feed the masses than to keep them hanging around starving.

He clapped his hands in a simple rhythm. "All right, everyone, let's pray and then we can eat."

The room stilled and the stragglers from the edges of the room pressed in.

Dave waited until everyone was settled before clasping his hands and bowing his head. "Heavenly Father, thank You for the meal that Jillian has prepared for us tonight. Thanks for bringing us all here safely—and for helping those of us who are going to be a little late to still arrive in time for the weeks of training ahead. Be with Margaret and Herb as they deal with her broken leg. Help us to handle the lack of Margaret and her skills during our time together. Most of all, Lord, we ask You to keep us solidly in Your will. Help us to seek it. To know it. And to walk inside it. Always. In Your name we pray, Amen." He opened his eyes and looked up before stepping back, so he wouldn't get trampled. "All right. Let the ladies go to the buffet line first, then everyone dig in."

Movement in the back caught his attention and he smiled. He pushed through the crowd and came to stand beside Elise. "You made it."

"I'm sorry I was late. You pray beautifully."

"Thanks." He held her gaze and didn't analyze the increase in his heart rate. "I didn't think you were going to come."

"I almost didn't." She sighed. "My daughters ganged up on me."

"Daughters?" He lifted his eyebrows.

"All three. Indigo called Jade and Skye. They cornered me."

"But Jade . . ."

"I know. It's confusing from the outside." Elise shrugged. "I didn't deal with her arrival on the scene very well, I'll admit that. But now? She might as well be my own daughter. I love her the same as I do the others. So I say I only have five, but Skye's not wrong when she says six."

"God is a God who restores."

Elise nodded. "He is."

"It's one of my favorite things to see." He gestured to the food line. "Why don't we fix our plates? I'm glad you came."

"Thanks." Her murmur held a question that he didn't know how to answer. He just knew he wanted her here with him for dinner. And helping out at the camp. And maybe as a friend.

That was all it could be. Dave was realistic enough to understand that. He'd had a good, long life with his wife, Mary. He had no regrets on that score. And it was greedy to ask for more. He was content with the blessings God had given him.

But he could always use another friend.

Elise put tiny helpings of everything on her plate. Dave followed behind, much more generous with his scoops. Jillian had been right—there was plenty. Everyone was through the line and there was enough, by his eye at least, for second helpings for anyone who might want them.

"You can have more than that, if you want." Dave nodded at her plate.

"I'm good. Thank you." Elise turned and surveyed the dining area.

Dave followed suit, smiling slightly when he found a two-person table in the corner of the room. The only one currently unoccupied. He nudged her with his elbow and pointed. "Why don't we sit over there? You can tell me how your praying went."

Elise sighed, but started in the direction of the little table. She set her plate down and sat, frowning at the food.

Dave set his plate down. "I'll go get us some lemonade and silverware."

"I can—"

"Just relax. I'll be right back." She was used to doing for herself, that much was obvious. That could be a good thing. Independence was always attractive. Right until it ran into stubbornness. He filled two glasses from the pitcher and snagged two sets of rolled flatware. "Here we are."

"Thank you." Elise flashed one of her sweet smiles before looking back down and unrolling her fork and knife.

"So? Did you get any clear leading?"

Dave picked up his sloppy joe and took a big bite. Jillian was quite the cook. Not that it was a gourmet dish, but he'd been around some folks who could still manage to mess them up. Jillian hadn't.

Elise picked at the top of her bun. "I don't know how to answer that. I told you I'm new to this."

He swallowed, nodding. "Okay. Did you get any clear feeling that it was something you shouldn't do? That it was wrong or that there was something else you should do instead? Maybe take Wayne and Betsy up on their offer to fly you out to see your other daughter?"

"They told you about that?" Her cheeks blazed bright red. "They had no business doing that. It's bad enough I'm here, dependent on their charity and goodness. I have a right not to get further in debt to them."

That was more than he'd expected. "So it's just pride keeping you here?"

"No." She blew out a breath. "I don't know how to explain it. It just doesn't sit well to take their money—again—just to see Azure. We video call all the time. I talk to my granddaughter. Maybe I don't get to hug them, but this works. They're busy and I'm . . . well, I'm here. And it's okay."

"Okay." He drew the word out, thinking through the best approach. "Do you think it's possible then, that not being willing to take their money and not feeling it's right to spend your own means God wants you at the ranch for a specific purpose?"

"You sound like the girls." She frowned and stabbed a bite of salad on her fork. "That's almost word for word what they said."

He grinned. "That's God."

"It probably is, isn't it?" Elise put down her fork and met his gaze. "I think you're making a huge mistake. I just want to go on record with that."

"All right." She was going to say yes. He could feel it. The jubilation in his soul couldn't all be from the relief that his ladies would have a confidant. But he'd worry about that another time. Sometime much, much later than now.

"If you're sure, then yes. I'll do it. Indigo thought it might be okay if I brought the spinning wheel over here so I'd have something to keep me occupied."

"That sounds great. Whatever you want. You're more than welcome to join us on the obstacle course or in the activities."

"Oh. No, thank you. I'm not what people consider

outdoorsy." Elise smiled. "In my younger years, sure, I didn't mind adventure. The older I've gotten, the more I've realized how grateful I am for the men and women who discovered how to make creature comforts work."

Dave laughed. That sounded like Mary. "The offer stands."

Elise nodded and cut off a bite of sloppy joe. "I don't anticipate changing my mind."

"Okay." He focused on his food for a few minutes. The campers were all chatting in their little groups. He didn't know the players yet, but it was always interesting to him to see the initial clusters as they formed and then watch as they changed and solidified over time. Not every pairing worked out. Generally, there wasn't any rancor between them, but sometimes it happened.

"Maybe you could explain a little more about what you're expecting." Elise pushed food around on her plate before setting her fork down and folding her hands in her lap. "I don't walk around with a pocketful of sage advice."

"Who does?" He grinned at her. "It's as simple—and as complicated—as being available for the women who are having a hard time or just need a listening ear. Sometimes people get homesick. Or they start to question if this is really what God wants them to be doing. Or—"

"Oh, now, wait." Elise paled and glanced around the room. "I don't know about helping people understand what God is or isn't calling them to do. I haven't even figured that out for myself. I know Betsy has to have told you I haven't been a believer all that long. Maybe I'm not the right person for this job after all. My daughter Skye would be a much better fit."

He reached over and covered one of her hands. He probably shouldn't have touched her—for any number of reasons—but he hadn't been able to stop himself, either. "Can you pray with someone?"

"Of course. Maybe not professionally."

He hid a smile. "What do you mean?"

"I mean I'm still new at this. I don't always have the words—my prayers aren't full of Scripture or fancy ideas."

"They don't need to be. They just need to be heartfelt."

She bit her lip and sighed. "I can do heartfelt. Are they going to want to talk to me, though?"

"Why wouldn't they?"

"They don't know me. I'm nobody."

"They wouldn't have known Margaret, either." He frowned. Why was she already trying to back out? "If you're really uncomfortable I guess I can try to find someone else. As much as I've enjoyed my few interactions with Skye, I think it's better to have someone with a little more life experience. And maybe not so close in age."

Elise's lips curved. "Older, you mean? Like me."

"There's something to be said for experience."

"I'm not sure the experience I have to offer is the kind you're looking for. You don't know me or the life I've lived. I'm not some paragon of virtue." Elise looked away. "I'm not special."

"Hey." He waited until she looked back at him. The naked pain on her face broke his heart. "I'm not looking for a paragon. Neither are they. They just need a kind heart and listening ears. Maybe a shoulder to cry on."

"I can do that. I'm scared."

"Doing something new is hard."

She laughed. "So much of life is. All right. I'll stop thinking up obstacles and give it my best. But if people complain or it seems like I'm not doing the job right, I expect you to be honest with me."

"I can do that." It was virtually impossible to do the job wrong. Not everyone would take advantage of a chance to talk with Elise—but Dave had a feeling that she was going to be wonderful. Was it wishful thinking? Maybe. Or maybe it was a nudge from the Holy Spirit.

"Promise me."

"I promise. But I'm also sure that you're going to be great." He glanced out at the group. Most had finished eating and were shifting in their seats. He hadn't given any instructions for after supper, so it made sense that there were nerves starting to show. He pushed his chair back and clapped his hands as he stood. "Can I get everyone's attention? If you're still finishing up, just keep on eating, but I thought I'd go over some announcements."

What little chatter there had been died out. Dave nodded.

"First up, I hope you're all settled in your rooms. Again, don't get too attached to them, as we aren't staying long. Tonight for sure and, depending on when the last group arrives, maybe tomorrow as well to give them a chance to breathe a minute after their traveling ordeal."

A few chuckles rolled around the room.

"You all have been communicating with Margaret as part of the pre-camp process. Unfortunately, she's not going to join us at all. Please keep her in your prayers. They're saying she might need surgery, but of course we'd all much rather she didn't. Either way, please pray for God's healing and comfort."

Here and there people nodded. Dave smiled. They were a good group—definitely on the serious side. That wasn't all bad. He turned and gestured to Elise, who seemed to be trying to shrink into invisibility.

"This is Elise Hewitt. She lives here at the ranch and has agreed to step in as mentor for the women. Elise, why don't you tell us all a little about yourself?" Dave sat back down and gestured for her to go ahead. The look she sent him was a cross between a deer in the headlights and something that definitely would have wounded him if it had been a physical weapon.

Elise rose and cleared her throat. She gave a little wave. "Hi.

Um. I'm Elise, like Dave said. The Hewitts—Wayne and Betsy—
who own Hope Ranch are my in-laws. Their son, Martin, and I
had five children together. And I have a bonus daughter who
shares Martin as her father."

Dave watched the crowd. There were some raised eyebrows,
but no one looked overly shocked. That was good. It didn't do
for anyone to be immediately judgmental. Ever, really, but
certainly not in a situation like this.

"I'm not sure what else to tell you. I'm happy to be a listening
ear as you need it. I never mind a good, strong hug." She
managed a faint smile. "And my kids—my daughters in particular—have said that I sometimes actually do know what I'm
talking about. I figure that counts pretty high when it comes to
kids and their mom."

The chuckles in the room were louder. Dave grinned. It was
high praise indeed for kids to be willing to admit that about a
parent.

"If I can get a list of names from Dave, I'm going to start
praying for each of you by name tonight. I can't imagine
embarking on this kind of journey myself, and I think that
you're all brave and amazing for even considering it. I hope that
God uses your time here to solidify His calling on your life."
Elise glanced at Dave and he gave her two thumbs up.

He was so proud of her. She hadn't let any of her nerves or
reservations about doing the job show, and Dave wanted to pull
her close and give her one of those good, strong hugs. Now
wasn't the time or the place for that, though. He stood again.
"Thanks, Elise. We're going to get her set up and comfy here in
the main lodge area. She helps one of her daughters with the
yarn shop over on the main part of the property, so she has
plenty of handwork to keep her busy. But if she's not meeting
with someone else, ladies, I want you to feel free to find her

when you need her. Just do let me know so I don't get worried that something bad has happened to you, okay?"

Elise laughed.

"Now, we have Jillian here to cook for us, but cleaning isn't her job. So when you're finished, please scrape your plates into the trash can and then carry them into the kitchen. We'll need some volunteers to wash and dry the dishes. Another set of hands will put things away as they're dried, and one more group to wash down the tables."

"Someone should put the leftovers away in the fridge and sweep this room." Elise shrunk back after she spoke.

Dave pointed at her and smiled. "That's a good point. Thank you. We'll need two people on food storage and then a sweeper. Whoever's sweeping should wait until the tables get wiped down to start. When you've completed your task and offered to help with anything that's taking a while, go have a seat in the lounge area. We'll gather there for vespers and an overview of tomorrow."

Noise and conversation picked up as Dave took his seat again.

"You don't think you should make assignments?" Elise brushed crumbs from the table into her hand and dusted them onto her plate.

"I'll let them figure it out tonight. If it doesn't work, then we'll deal with it in a more organized fashion tomorrow. Do you really want a list of names?"

Her eyebrows lifted. "I do. Why would I have said I did if I didn't?"

"I don't know. I think it's a lovely thing—just the kind of thing Margaret would do." He took out his phone and tapped on the screen. "Can I get your email address?"

"Oh. Of course. It's Elise H at Hope Ranch dot com."

"Yeah? That's nice."

"The Hewitts are nothing but nice."

"That bothers you?"

"No. No, I appreciate it. I just feel beholden, I guess. I don't like it, particularly." Elise shrugged. "I'll get over it."

"Good."

"Really?"

He nodded and finished tapping the screen. "You should have the names in an email. And yes, it's good, because people do nice things, and it's always better to say thank you than to look for the hidden poison."

"It's not that I'm looking for poison, so much as I don't like feeling as though I don't do anything to contribute to my upkeep. I don't guess I expect you to understand."

Dave laughed. "Oh, but I do. What do you think missionary life is like? Mary and I spent years living off the charity of others. They paid so that we could take Jesus to others. It's hard, I'll admit, but the friendships I've made with donors over the years have made one thing very clear: people consider it a privilege to help. And it's wrong of me to deprive them of the opportunity because of my pride."

7

Afternoon sunshine slanted through the windows of the lodge. Elise stopped the spinning wheel and shook her hands out to dispel the cramping. Or at least try. So far, no one had shown up to talk to her. Dave had told her this morning that it would probably be a few days. So she wasn't going to worry about it.

His words from the night before stuck with her and she'd turned them over in her mind off and on throughout the day. Did Betsy and Wayne consider it a privilege to help her? They always said it wasn't a problem and that they loved having her there, but Martin had always been so adamant that his parents weren't what everyone thought they were. Was she still letting him cloud her mind, even when the evidence of her own experience was the opposite?

"Hey, Mom." Skye wandered into the lounge area and flopped down on one of the sofas. "How's it going?"

"Good. Quiet. You?"

"The same. It's odd not having more groups on the schedule. I'm used to juggling pre-camp checklists with the needs of the current campers. Now that Dave's booked the next two months, I have a lot of downtime."

"Is that bad?"

"No. Just different. More time to read." She grinned.

Elise chuckled. "You were always one for a good book. Maybe you can dig through the pile of comp copies Jade's been stockpiling from the Christian authors she works with. I've read a handful. They're not what I expected."

"Better or worse?"

"Definitely better." Elise frowned. "I'd gotten it in my head that Christian anything was a lesser shadow of the 'real' version."

"That's Dad. He gets in my head sometimes, too. I get so mad when I think of Wayne and Betsy and how Dad kept us away from them—and them away from us—for no reason other than the fact that they loved Jesus."

"It was a little more than that." Elise had never shared all the details she had about Martin's decision to leave the ranch. It wasn't her story to tell. Or, maybe it was, now that Martin was gone. But it didn't change anything. Even with the full information, Elise didn't see where he'd had any of it right. "He didn't like their rules. And they didn't like his rebellion—so they added more rules. It just kept escalating. So he left. He was wrong to do it. And I wish I'd pushed harder for him to fix things with them when you kids were younger."

Skye took Elise's hand. "I love that you tried, Mom. It wasn't worth more fighting though. You needed to protect your relationship with him, too."

Elise nodded. That had been her thought. Maybe, looking back, it had been wrong. But Elise hadn't wanted to risk Martin's leaving for good. He wouldn't have taken the kids. He wouldn't have shared responsibility for them, either. And how was Elise supposed to care for five kids as a single mom with no job skills?

So she'd compromised. And settled. And made the choices that seemed reasonable at the time.

She couldn't regret it. Not fully. But not wanting to repeat the mistakes of her past made it hard to know how to step into the future. She didn't have a good track record when it came to decision making.

"So. Dave."

Elise looked at her daughter, frowning slightly. "What about him?"

"He's a silver fox, don't you think?"

"Skye!"

"What? I'm not blind, Mom, and he's hot. You can't tell me you didn't notice."

"You're married. You shouldn't be noticing. Plus he's older than your father." And older than Elise, for that matter. Not that seven years was a big deal at their age. "And he's married, too, for that matter."

"Widowed."

Elise lifted a shoulder. It was a small distinction. The way Dave talked about Mary made it clear that they'd loved each other well. And that he still loved her even though she was gone.

"Any idea what happened there?"

"No. I didn't ask. I don't need to get to know him to do the missionary women a favor."

The disappointment on Skye's face was almost comical. "Oh, Mom."

"What?"

"Don't you want someone to spend the rest of your life with?"

What life? She was past that, wasn't she? "I had that, honey. For all our problems, your father was a good man. A good partner. And now I'm just too old."

"You're only fifty-three. You have a lot of years ahead of you. You deserve to be happy."

"No one deserves happiness. I understand what you're saying, but Jesus doesn't promise us happiness. He just says He'll be with us. And I'm trying to learn to be content where I am. This seems to be where I've been planted, so I'd like to figure out how to bloom." That was the whole point behind the Apostle Paul's thing about being able to do all things, wasn't it? Being content where God had put him, regardless of the circumstance. So it was what Elise would try to do, too.

Skye was frowning at her. Almost scowling. "I still think—"

"Don't think, honey, okay?" Elise rubbed Skye's leg. "I'm fine. There are worse things in life than having a place like this to live out the rest of my days. And if Indigo keeps making more headway with her yarn, we've talked about how I can help and earn a little spending money so I'm not relying on your grandparents and the little bit I have saved."

"You should have gone to see Azure with Grandma."

Elise shook her head. "No. It didn't sit right. Still doesn't. And now Dave has this job for me, so maybe this is what God wanted all along."

"And you're okay with it?"

"What's the alternative? It's fine. And if things keep going like they have today? No one is going to come to talk to me, so it's just a different place for me to hang out. If nothing else, it's a chance for Indigo to see how she does with baby Elise on her own all day."

Skye laughed. "She misses you."

Elise bit her lip. Was this actually a bad idea? "I can probably still help out. There's no reason I couldn't set up the playpen and keep an eye."

"Mom, chill. Indigo's fine. And if it gets to be too hard,

Wayne has already volunteered to come and help out. Joaquin, too."

Elise nodded. Of course. She wasn't indispensible. She wasn't supposed to be. "That's good, then. I guess I'll let her know that we can figure something out here, too, if she needs an additional option."

"I'm sure she'd be happy to hear it." Skye paused a moment. "Are you okay?"

"What do you mean? Of course, I am." Elise didn't meet Skye's searching gaze. Her daughter was too insightful sometimes. But she wasn't supposed to be a burden to her daughter, and she was fine. Or fine enough. "Have you and Morgan given any thought to adding to my growing number of grandchildren?"

Skye laughed. "No. Not yet. You have five. Isn't that enough for now?"

"I suppose." Elise hid a grin. At least it had made her daughter stop prodding into Elise's life. "But I want more. And since I don't get to see Azure and Matt very often, those of you who are here will have to make up the difference."

"Four of the five are here at the ranch." Skye shook her head. "I see what you're doing. I'll let it go for now, but Mom? Don't close yourself off. You're not old. There's a lot of life still ahead of you."

"That's not guaranteed, and you know it." Martin had been the same age and he was gone.

"Mom . . ."

"Don't, honey. It's okay. I'm fine. You worry too much."

Skye snorted, but stood. "I love you."

"I love you, too. Go organize something." Elise winked. "I'm going to try and get more of this roving spun so I have something to show for my time today."

"Because Indigo is a hard taskmaster." Skye's rolling eyes emphasized the sarcasm dripping from her words.

"Maybe not, but I'd still like to do more." Elise gave the spinning wheel a little push and started feeding roving to the spindle. Her feet picked up the rhythm easily—she was definitely getting the hang of this. She could feel Skye watching her, but didn't look over. Elise was okay. She didn't need a new man in her life. She didn't need adventures. She'd had a good, full life, and being out to pasture wasn't all bad.

"Do you maybe want to come for dinner tonight? It's nothing fancy—just chicken Caesars—but there's plenty. I know Morgan would enjoy seeing you."

"How about a rain check?" Elise glanced over at her daughter and smiled. "I think, after today, I'm going to be ready for a little time at home."

"Okay. But I'm going to hold you to that." Skye rubbed Elise's shoulder. "I guess I'll go to the office and see if there's anything I should be doing."

"Bye, hon." Elise slowly let out her breath as Skye wandered off. How pathetic was it that her children were worried about her?

Elise lost herself in the rhythmic repetition of feeding wool onto the spindle and watching it twist into yarn. She'd need to ply this—probably a three-ply would be best given how thin it was turning out—but it wasn't nearly as bumpy and homespun-looking as her drop spindle efforts always seemed.

"I don't think I've ever watched spinning for any length of time."

Elise jolted at Dave's voice and reached out to stop the wheel.

"Sorry. I didn't mean for you to stop." He had a boyish grin and stood with his hands tucked in his pockets.

"It's fine. You're done for the day?" She didn't see the campers, but that didn't necessarily mean anything.

"Nearly. They're out there finishing up a teambuilding exercise before dinner. Can you join us again?"

A refusal hovered on the tip of her tongue. She'd turned down Skye and meant what she'd said about not wanting company. Even after a day basically alone in the lodge, she was exhausted and ready for the quiet of home.

"It's spaghetti pie. I don't know if that adds to the temptation to come or encourages you to stay away, but I'd really enjoy it if you'd stay."

She closed her eyes. She had no defense against that puppy dog look that attractive men all seemed to possess. Martin had always been able to get his way with it. Now, it seemed that Dave had learned to sing off the same sheet of music. She sighed. "What's the side?"

"Garlic bread and a mixed salad."

It was better than anything she was going to whip up in her cabin by leaps and bounds. "All right. Thank you."

He grinned. "I feel like that's my line."

Elise chuckled.

"So what happens after this?" Dave pointed to the spinning wheel. "Is it ready to be sold?"

"It can be. But I think with this I'll split it into thirds and then spin them together to make it a thicker weight. That'll be more versatile in terms of the sorts of projects that someone could use it for."

"You won't use it?"

Elise shook her head. "I have too many projects started already. I don't need another just now. And I think Indigo has someone in mind for this, but I can't honestly remember for certain. I just know she needs it spun, and it was something that I could do to occupy my hands while I'm here."

Dave perched on the arm of the sofa so he was at eye level. "I really appreciate your willingness to do this for me. For the ladies."

Heat seared her cheeks. It was the intensity of his gaze. Knowing that didn't do anything to slow her heart or cool her face, though. "It's no bother."

"It is. I know it is." He paused and seemed to be organizing his thoughts. "Would you be willing to plan on dinner here with us on the nights we're at the lodge? And you could stay for our devotional time."

"I don't think—"

"It's not much more. Tonight. Tomorrow. Then we're camping for the next eight days, so we won't be around. The ladies will still have free rein to seek you out as needed, but dinner will be what we put together over a campfire. I think if you're here for Bible study and prayer, it will help."

Why did he have to make sense? The women were much more likely to see her as someone they could—or should—talk to if she was someone they actually knew. Even if they only knew her a little, it would be better than the expectation that they bare their soul to a random stranger. "Yeah. Okay. Do I— would it be better if I did the camping stuff with you?"

"I love that you'd ask that, but no. I don't think so. Margaret never has—she says she's paid her dues." Dave chuckled. "And having a chance to get away from camp and get into the air conditioning is a good excuse for some of the women."

"Okay." She let her breath whoosh out. It was a relief, no question. She would have done it if Dave had said it was better, but she would have spent a lot of the time asking God just what He was thinking. Maybe she wasn't supposed to do that, but she couldn't quite stop the questions sometimes. "So. How did your day go today?"

"Really well. The obstacle course is amazing. The guys who

built it exceeded my expectations."

"That's fantastic. Joaquin and Tommy had a lot of fun building it—I know they'd love to hear your thoughts about it if you get a minute."

"Maybe I could walk you back to your cabin after devotions this evening and you could point them out."

Elise looked away. Was he hitting on her? Surely not. "I'll be fine. It's not dangerous around here."

"No snakes?" He winked.

She shivered. "Not on the paths. Usually. Honestly, the one on Sunday was the first I've seen since I've been here."

"That's good. I've been a little worried, wondering if we're going to run into them constantly while we're out camping. Still, if you don't mind me walking you back, I'd be happy to do it."

"If you have the time, I won't say you can't."

He chuckled. "If that's the best I can get, then I'll take it."

Footsteps and chatter grew louder. The door opened, and the bulk of the campers came through in groups of twos, threes, and fours. Many of them lifted a hand in greeting or paused to say hello on their way through the main lodge sitting area.

Elise watched as they headed toward the stairs. They looked happy. Excited. And impossibly young.

"I think they get younger every year." Dave's head was shaking.

Elise laughed. "I was just thinking that. Well, not the every year thing—I'm not sure I was ever that young."

He cocked his head to the side, his study of her verging on disconcerting. "I imagine by the time you were in your mid-twenties like them, you already had three of your babies and were handling the mom thing with aplomb. Did you work outside the home while they were growing up?"

Elise blinked. Her cheeks warmed. "I don't know about any aplomb, but you're right about the kids. Azure, Cyan, and Indigo would all have been clinging to my legs by then. We would've been living on the bus at that point."

"The bus?"

"I'm surprised no one told you." It seemed like he knew everything there was to know about her. "Martin—he was Wayne and Betsy's son—never had a lot of time for conventional. He decided it was easier to move from place to place following the work if we could take our house with us. He found a school bus for sale, did some work converting it into something livable, and we were set."

"A school bus."

He was staring at her now. "What?"

"I'm trying to picture it."

"I don't think you'll ever turn it into something that fits. I didn't love it, but it worked well enough. The kids turned out okay, at least. Better than I probably have the right to expect."

"I imagine most parents feel that way."

"Do you have children?"

Dave shook his head, his eyes clouding. "No. Not in the traditional sense. Mary was never able to sustain a pregnancy past a month or two. Some of that is probably where we were living, although there are plenty of jungle missionaries who manage to have and raise families all while serving the Lord. But Mary was the honorary mother or grandmother to so many of the tribe's children that it kept her busy. After a while, we both adjusted."

"I'm sorry." What would that be like? So much of her life had been consumed by her children. She wanted it that way—wouldn't have changed it for the world—and the empty nest when Royal and Skye had spread their wings had been harder to deal with than either she or Martin had anticipated.

"Don't be. God took care of us. And like I said, we had children in the families we served who loved us." He cleared his throat. "Did you live in the bus after the kids left home?"

"For a little while. A year? Maybe two. Then we realized we were happy in Arizona, so Martin decided to sell the bus and buy a house." And she'd let him handle all the details, because that was what he had wanted. She didn't care. Not really. The bus was fine. The house was fine. But if she'd realized how he'd overextended them, she would never have agreed to it. "That was lovely, too. We didn't get to know the neighbors as well as I'd hoped, because Martin never really moved past the 'we're only here temporarily' mindset. I suspect, if he'd lived, he would have wanted to get back on the road again."

"How did he die?" He bit off the words and reached out to touch her arm. "I'm sorry. You don't have to tell me."

"It's not a secret." It would have been nice if there were any possibility of keeping it quiet, but that wasn't how Wayne and Betsy operated. They didn't hide the shameful parts. Maybe it was for the best, but it still grated now and again. Elise cleared her throat and focused on the trees outside the window. "I told you Martin was unconventional."

He nodded.

"And I think I mentioned we were never legally married. There were many times when he'd park the bus somewhere that made a good home for me and the kids, and then he'd take off to work in an area that was less safe. He'd be gone weeks—sometimes months—at a time. And our agreement was that as long as he didn't have another family, he could do what he wanted while he was away." She glanced back at him.

Dave's eyes were wide, his eyebrows raised.

She offered a tight smile. "I did mention I was new to believing in Jesus, didn't I?"

"You did. I shouldn't be shocked. It's not that it's hard to believe people make that choice—I just don't understand why anyone would ask that of you."

She frowned. Why wouldn't they? She shrugged. "I guess, in

my heart, I knew it was possible that he had other children out there. And it turned out that he did. When Skye and Royal asked about it—they'd done a DNA test for one of Royal's social media sponsorships, and Jade was in there—it set off an avalanche of problems that resulted in Martin having an aneurysm."

"I'm so sorry."

"Thanks. He actually recovered, somewhat, from that. Then a few months later we had an argument, he took off, and he ended up having a heart attack when there was no one around to get him help." She looked back out the window. The breeze was making the branches full of pine needles sway. "So he died. I ended up here. In the end, I'm grateful the Hewitts took me in, showed me Jesus, and kept me as part of their family. They didn't have to, by any stretch of the imagination. And most of the time I can keep from wondering if Martin had ever accepted Jesus. Will I see him again? Or is he suffering eternal torment because he was too stubborn to soften his heart and accept the truth he was raised in?"

Dave took her hand and gave it a gentle squeeze. "Have you talked to the Hewitts about that?"

"No." She didn't pull her hand away. She wanted to flip it over and lace her fingers through his, but she fought that back. She'd known Dave for what, five days? Which basically meant she didn't know him at all. Now she did tug her hand free. "There's no point in making them sad, too."

"They might not be sad. Maybe they could tell you about a time in his life when Martin asked Jesus to be his savior."

Elise looked at Dave and felt the scowl form on her face. "Do you really believe someone can be saved and then go on to live a life committed to rebelling against Jesus? I am sure there was a time when Martin said the words his parents expected him to say. I just don't think they ever moved past his lips and into his heart. His life—at least for the years I knew him—was never one that I could point to and say, 'There's someone who knows Jesus.' Not one instance comes to mind."

Dave blew out a breath. "Well. I guess you have to leave it in God's hands. He knows what Martin's heart truly was."

Elise nodded. If she got to heaven and ran into Martin, she'd be stunned. The Bible was pretty clear that believers couldn't go on about their life continuing to sin whenever they wanted. But maybe there was something she hadn't read yet. Or understood. There was a lot about living for Jesus that she didn't necessarily understand. She was just doing her best. "It doesn't matter in the long term. It's not as if I can change anything—or as if knowing one way or the other would change anything. It's between Martin and Jesus."

"That's true." Dave looked as though he was going to add more, but his mouth snapped shut as Jillian hurried into the lounge.

"Hi. Do you have kitchen helpers today? I could use a hand."

"I'll come." Elise stood and scooted past Dave's knees.

"I can help, too." Dave started to rise.

"Oh, one's great for now." Jillian glanced at her watch. "But if you and maybe two others want to help set up the buffet line in about twenty minutes, I won't say no."

"Okay." Dave eased back onto the sofa. "Can I slide the spinning wheel over against the wall, Elise?"

"Sure. Thanks. I guess it's kind of in the way where it is."

"Not at all. I just don't want someone to mess it up. You go help Jillian. I'll see you at supper."

"Thanks so much, Mrs. Hewitt."

"It's Elise, Jillian. Please?" She followed behind the young woman and tried not to look over her shoulder. Dave was watching her leave. She couldn't decide if that was good or bad.

8

"Is my mom gone?" Skye peered around the corner before entering the room fully.

Dave pointed toward the kitchen. "She's helping Jillian with dinner."

"Oh, good. That should keep her occupied for a minute or two." Skye dragged a chair close to the couch and sat. "Can I ask you a personal question?"

Dave's eyebrows lifted. "You can ask. I won't promise to answer."

"Fair enough." Skye grinned. "Do you like my mom?"

"Do I like your mom? In what way? She seems like a lovely woman."

"Is that it?"

"I'm not sure what you're getting at." He might have a little idea. At the same time, he wasn't comfortable even thinking about his feelings. He certainly didn't want to discuss them with Elise's daughter.

"Gosh, the two of you are a pair. Look, you can tell me it's none of my business and I'll leave it alone. Or you can be straight with me and I'll help you. Indigo and Jade are on board, too."

"On board. What, exactly, are you suggesting? Be clear. Maybe use small words."

"You. And my mom." Skye grinned and leaned forward eagerly. "Look, Dad died two years ago. Mom's . . . drifting. She doesn't act like she has a purpose and that's just not like her. I think it's because she was fighting with Dad when he died, so she's feeling guilty. Whatever it is, she deserves better. She's young, ish, and I just want her to be happy."

"I'm not sure where I come in." Dave didn't necessarily want to know where he came in. Elise was pretty. Attractive. But also? A distraction. He had a call on his life and somehow, he didn't see Elise as the kind of up-to-her-elbows-right-along-with-him girl that Mary had been. "Happiness isn't everything. And no one can make someone happy. That's a choice we all make on our own."

Skye laughed and slapped her knee. "Honestly, you're perfect for her. She gave me a mini lecture about happiness too. And I get that. I really do. And yet, I want it for her."

"That speaks well of you. I think your mother is capable of finding her own happiness." Elise struck him as a competent woman on top of everything else.

"Not if she isn't looking." Skye frowned. "Never mind. Just forget I said anything."

"Do you honestly believe your mother is interested in any sort of relationship?" Because he hadn't gotten that feeling from Elise. At all. Maybe it had been too long since he last had to try to understand women—because it had, in fact, been a long time. But he didn't remember it being quite this hard.

Skye sighed. "I believe she needs one. That she'll be happier with one. I also don't think she believes she deserves anything more than she's already had."

"I'll tell you what. I'll keep getting to know your mom, and we can see what happens."

"Will you pray about it, too?"

He smiled. "I already have been."

Skye laughed. "See? I knew you liked her."

"Which doesn't mean we're meant to be together. Don't get your hopes up too high, okay? Your mom knows her own mind. And she's entitled to live her life the way she feels God is leading her. My life? This work I do? It's not easy, even if I'm not in the mission field full time anymore. She may decide she's just not equipped for it. And that's okay." The main thing he pushed when he did these camps was finding God's will and living in the center of it. Everyone who loved Jesus should want to live in the center of His will, whether or not they wanted to be a missionary. "You said your sisters were in on this?"

Skye nodded.

"Then the three of you need to pray about it. Together and alone. Pray for your mom. Pray for me."

"Okay. You should know that Wayne thinks it's a good idea, too."

"Your grandfather? You talked to him about this?" This family had different boundaries than what he was used to. His own parents were in their mid-eighties and, for the most part, left him completely alone. He spoke to them on the phone once or twice a week when he was in a place where that was possible. But beyond that? They would never have offered an opinion about his romantic life unsolicited. Probably not even if he asked what they thought. Mary's folks, before they'd passed, had been much the same way.

"Talking to you was actually Grandpa's idea. He didn't think it was good to leave you both in the dark if we were going to try to nudge the two of you together."

Dave shook his head.

"Thanks, Mr. Fitzgerald." Skye stood.

"Don't thank me yet. You don't know how this is going to work out."

Skye shrugged. "I have a good feeling. Make sure you let me know if you need anything while you're here."

"We're heading out on the mountain tomorrow. Planning on a couple-hour hike before we set up camp. So you won't be seeing as much of me—or the group—until Wednesday."

"You're staying out there a week?" Skye shuddered. "I can't fathom camping for that long. What if—"

"I'll have my cell phone for emergencies. I have your number and Wayne's programmed in. It has a solar charger, so it shouldn't be an issue. Wayne assured me that there ought to be a signal." That was iffy, as far as Dave was concerned, but Wayne had seemed very sure. Worst case, he'd have to hike back a little until the thing worked.

"All right. Be safe."

"That's the plan." Dave watched Skye wander off before leaning back. What an unexpected conversation. His thoughts might have been tending in that direction, but he certainly hadn't been getting much—any?—encouragement from Elise. He didn't want to push her. If Martin had only been gone two years, maybe it was too soon. They'd had a lot of years together, just like he and Mary had.

Cancer had taken Mary five years ago. Some mornings he woke up and it hurt like she'd passed the day before. Other days, the pain was dulled. It never went completely away. Elise might not be the only one who wasn't ready to move on. He'd pray about that, too.

But the truth was, Elise was the first woman since Mary who'd caught his eye.

A group of four campers clattered down the stairs.

"Hi, Dave. When's dinner? It smells good." The first guy—

was it Logan? That sounded right, at least—stopped in front of him.

Dave checked his watch. "Let's go see if we can help get the buffet line setup. Jillian should be about ready for us."

The other guy in the group slugged Logan's arm. "Nice, man. Now we have to help."

"Get to, I think you mean?" Dave shot the young man a steely glare. That one was George, and he was already a pain in Dave's backside. If he had to write final recommendations right now? George wasn't getting a positive one. He had no business on the mission field. He was self-centered and clearly only interested in hooking up with as many women as possible. Dave hadn't thought the lack of Herb was something he was even going to notice, but an extra set of eyes on George would've been a big help. As it was, Dave would assign himself as George's buddy. That should stop the majority of the shenanigans, even if it did cramp Dave's experience.

"Yeah, yeah. Get to." George's eyes rolled in an exaggerated manner. "It's worse than being at my mom's house."

"George. Why don't you hang here a moment while your friends go get started."

George hesitated, but ultimately seemed to recognize that Dave's words weren't actually a question, regardless of how they'd been phrased.

"Have a seat." Dave gestured to the couch.

George glanced around before sitting in one of the nearby arm chairs.

"That's it. Go up to your room and pack. I'll call the airlines about rearranging your ticket." How much was a taxi or rideshare going to cost from here to Albuquerque? Dave frowned then dismissed the concern. George could figure that out. Maybe, if someone from the ranch was willing and able, he could set up something else, but even then, George was going to pay something.

"No. I'm here for two weeks. You can't send me home." George crossed his arms, belligerence scrawled across his features.

Dave moved until he stood with his toes a hair's breadth from George's. He leaned forward slightly, towering over the young man. "Yes, I can. Would you like me to call up the agency and have them remind you of the agreement you signed?"

George shifted uncomfortably in his seat. "I don't remember reading anything about being able to get sent home."

"How much of the paperwork did you actually read?" Dave cocked his head to the side. The boy was still scowling, but there were tinges of fear evident in his eyes.

George shrugged one shoulder. "I signed where my parents told me to sign."

"Then I guess, if nothing else, you've learned a valuable lesson about reading paperwork before agreeing to the terms. The short version is that you agreed to submit yourself to the disciplinary actions of the camp director." Dave tapped his chest. "That's me."

"So, what, I don't want to be on kitchen duty so I get sent home? That's stupid."

"It's not just kitchen duty, George. I've seen you hitting on the women. I've heard your off-color remarks about the ones who turn you down. And I've done my best to intercept anyone attempting to sneak away from the group so you can grope them in the forest. That's not what missionaries do. It's not the purpose of this camp. And if I had even the tiniest shred of belief that you were interested in dedicating your life to serving Jesus, I'd let you stay and we'd try to work through this as an attempt by Satan to keep you from fulfilling God's call on your life. But you don't feel called to mission work, do you?" Dave was vaguely aware of a small crowd gathering in the lounge. Maybe he should have taken George somewhere more private for this conversation. On the other hand, maybe it was good for everyone to realize that this was serious. Not just two weeks in the woods for grins and giggles.

George recoiled. "What? No. I don't want to be a missionary. But I also don't want my parents to disown me. This was one of the meager options they gave me."

Dave's heart hurt for the kid, but it wasn't safe to keep him here. He prayed for wisdom. "What were the other options?"

"Enlist in something military or enroll in the community college and live at home where they'd monitor my comings and goings and grades." George snorted. "Two weeks in the mountains sounded like the easiest choice."

"I can see how you'd feel that way. Unfortunately, you're wrong." Dave pinched the bridge of his nose. "You can't stay, George. This is a camp for people who are seriously considering mission work. Not everyone who finishes is going to follow through, and that's fine, but the understanding is that they're coming with the full intention of making this their life's work and spending that time seeking God. You just admitted you don't meet those criteria."

George scowled and looked away. "So you're just sending me home."

"Home. Or I can help you find a military recruiter—I'm sure there's one within an easy drive. I can get someone to take you there or the airport. Either way, you can't stay here."

"I thought Jesus was all about love."

Dave's lips quirked up. "He is. But it's not the kind of love that lets people do whatever they want. It's a lot like the love your parents have for you. Jesus wants His children to serve Him —to turn from sin and let Him transform them into His image.

It's love that comes with boundaries and discipline. Love that doesn't have those things? It's not really love."

"Whatever, man."

"Let's call the airline and see when we can get your flight changed to." Dave sighed. There was more he'd like to say, but the young man wasn't in a place where he'd be receptive to it. Maybe he never would be. "I'll be praying for you, George. Even though you won't be finishing out your time here with us."

George shrugged.

"Do you want to call your folks?" Dave slid his phone out and opened his email. He had information on all the flights in there somewhere. *Aha.* He tapped the email and scrolled to George's name.

"No. They'll just be angry. I can do without another lecture."

Dave moved to the couch and sat. He opened his browser app and put in the name of George's airline, then tapped the phone icon on the search results. As it rang, he glanced over at the gathered crowd and waved them toward the eating area. "Why don't you all go get settled. One of you can bless the meal and then everyone can get started. There's no point in holding things up while George and I take care of this."

George sank back into the cushions of his chair, his scowl deepening.

Dave didn't bother to sigh. George had obviously thought Dave was bluffing. But he wasn't. The airline customer service operator answered and Dave cleared his throat. "Yes, hello, I'd like to change a ticket."

9

"Happy birthday, baby girl." Elise bent down and scooped her namesake into her arms.

"Gamma! Cake!"

"That's right, we're having cake because you're a whole year old now." Elise kissed the little girl's button nose.

"Down!"

Elise laughed and let the toddler wiggle back to the floor, then watched as she ran off to the little play kitchen Betsy and Wayne had set up in their living room. Cyan and Maria's little girl, Cara, was already there. She'd turned one in July. The two of them were as close as siblings. Maybe closer.

"It's too bad Betsy's missing this." Wayne slung an arm companionably over Elise's shoulders.

"It is." And Elise was missing whatever fun Betsy was having with Azure, Matt, and Grace. "But it's good she was able to make the trip. And she'll be home on Monday, right?"

"She will." Wayne patted Elise's shoulder. "I can't help wishing you would've let us send you along with her."

"I know. And I appreciate the offer. Maybe," Elise had to

pause and swallow the nervous lump in her throat, "maybe next time. It's hard for me to take so much and give so little."

Wayne turned and held her gaze. "You give plenty."

Elise shrugged. She didn't. But she also knew she wasn't going to convince Wayne of that. So just smile and nod and move on. It was one of the ways she'd learned to deal with Martin when it was clear he was digging his heels in.

She nodded at her two granddaughters playing together. "The two of them get along so well. It's good to see."

"It is. And I imagine they'll have a little tussle over some of the gifts later, just like they did at Cara's party."

Elise laughed. "Probably. I just don't understand letting a toddler open gifts when other kids are around, but what do I know?"

"She has to learn to share at some point, Mom." Indigo joined them. She offered the platter of appetizers she held. "Eat something. Please. Maria's in the kitchen and there's enough food there. I'm pretty sure she thinks we invited the whole town."

"That sounds like Maria." Wayne scooped three stuffed mushrooms off the plate and cradled them in his hand. "I can't say I mind. It's good eating."

Elise took one of the mushrooms and a small triangle of toast covered in what looked like chopped up olives. "She has a gift. As for sharing, that'll come. I don't think having presents she can't touch dangled in front of her is the way to do it, but I'm old school. None of you even had a birthday party until you were five."

"Really?" Indigo's brow furrowed. "Huh. I guess I always assumed I didn't remember them because I was so young."

Wayne laughed. "Martin never had parties, either. When he was nine or so we started having a friend or two up for a sleep-over, but birthdays were usually low-key."

"I think this is lovely, though, Indigo. And it's just family. It's not like you *did* invite the whole town. So really, we're using baby Elise's birthday as an excuse to get together."

"Speaking of baby Elise." Indigo smiled. "Joaquin and I were talking—her name's getting to be a mouthful. Do you like Lissy or Lisa better as a nickname?"

"I like either one. You're her parents. You choose. I'll call her whatever you want." Elise watched her granddaughters playing. It would be good to have a nickname. She'd noticed people stumbling over there being two Elises, though context usually made it clear which Elise they meant.

"You have to break the tie. We can't decide." Indigo gripped Elise's arm.

Elise laughed. "Lissy, then. Or, maybe Leecey? So it has a little more of a clear tie to Elise?"

"Oh, I like that." Indigo grinned. "Let me go run it by Joaquin. That's why he's been pushing for Lisa. But you remember that girl Lisa we were always running into when I was what, eleven?"

Elise nodded. That had been Indigo's first—and worst—introduction to the world of mean girls. "I haven't thought of her in years."

"Yeah, well, I can't always keep her mean-spirited tongue out of my head even now. So I *really* don't want to call my baby girl Lisa."

"If your granddad's opinion matters at all, Leecey would be my vote as well." Wayne reached for the plate of appetizers. "It'll be easy enough to stop using when she's older and doesn't like the diminutive. Or if she doesn't care, it's not so babyish that she can't use it even as an adult."

Indigo chuckled. "Thanks, Grandpa."

"I wonder when they're going to officially start." Elise

glanced around the room, counting heads. "It seems like everyone's here."

The doorbell chimed.

Elise frowned.

"Maybe they invited some folks from church." Wayne thrust the plate toward her. "You hold this. I'll go get the door."

Elise took the food and frowned at it. After a moment, she popped another of the stuffed mushrooms into her mouth before sliding the plate onto the coffee table and wandering over to where Calvin was slouched on the sofa, his fingers working overtime on the controllers of his Nintendo Switch.

"Hi, Grandma." Calvin's glance flicked over to her then back to the screen.

Elise watched as characters from Mario zoomed around in cars and buggies, weaving between mushrooms and giant, toothy, bombs that clomped down onto the track, barking like dogs.

"You wanna play?" Calvin set the Switch on his lap as his car spun to a stop past the checkered finish line.

"Sure. You'll probably win."

Calvin grinned. "Yeah, I know. But it's fun, anyway."

Elise laughed and nudged his shoulder with her own. "Tell me what to do."

Calvin made short work of sliding the controllers off the screen and switching to a 2-player game. He frowned a moment before dragging a chair closer to prop the screen up with its little kickstand. "Can you see that okay?"

"Sure." Elise looked down at the tiny rectangle in her hand. Seeing the screen was the least of her problems. "Now what?"

"You have to choose your character." Calvin worked his controller, and a colored box scooted between the cartoon images. He settled on a turtle and pressed a button. "I like Yoshi."

"Are they different? Is one better?" Elise squinted at the controller, pressed a button, and grinned when the box moved like she'd thought it should. "Or can I just choose this one because she's a princess?"

Calvin rolled his eyes. "You can be the princess if you want. I never choose her."

Elise chuckled and tapped another button to select the princess.

"Now you scroll through the carts. They have different stats, see in the box?" Calvin pointed as he quickly spun through his options and confirmed them.

Elise wasn't going to sit and debate the relative merits of a baby buggy to a go-kart. She set hers to the same thing Calvin had chosen—he had to have a reason, didn't he?—and clicked the button.

"Cool. Ready, Grandma?"

"Ready as I'm going to be."

Calvin cackled.

Before long, the little guy in the cloud was counting down from three and Calvin's car had zoomed off down the track. Elise fumbled the controls for a few seconds before remembering them and taking off. She felt herself leaning as her character took the curves.

"Hit A, Grandma! Hit A!"

She did as Calvin instructed and her princess morphed into a bullet that sped around the course, passing up all but Calvin's cart, which was too far ahead for her to catch. She laughed. "That was fun."

"Keep going!"

She managed to hold on to second place, after Calvin but ahead of the computer-generated players, through two more laps.

"Way to go, Grandma. The next race is coming up, you ready?"

Elise set the controller in her lap and shook out her hands. "Can I have a second to recover? I'm not as young as you."

Calvin snickered. "Okay."

"Do you need something to eat?" Elise tried to keep her concern about Calvin's diabetes to a minimum. He had plenty of people who worried about him and she didn't want to add to that. It had to get old.

He wrinkled his nose, but reached for the combined insulin pump and continuous glucose monitor that was hooked at his waistband. He frowned at the display. "Yeah, I guess. I'll go find Mom. I want to finish this race though, okay?"

"Absolutely. I'm not going anywhere." She watched him set the Switch aside and scamper off toward the kitchen.

The couch dipped beside her and she glanced over. Her heart stuttered in her chest when her gaze landed on Dave.

"Hi."

She blinked. "What are you doing here?"

Dave laughed.

Her hand flew to her mouth. "I'm sorry. I'm just surprised."

"It's okay." His head angled to the side. "Indigo invited me. The campers are busy with lean-to construction this morning, so it was nice to get away. There are a couple of them that seem to need my approval for every move they make. It gets old. And it's not beneficial to them. They have to learn to figure it out and be confident in their decisions."

"Sure. I can see that." Sort of. They were still learning. "They don't need supervision?"

Dave shook his head. "They should be fine. I'll be back in time to look things over before they have to sleep in the beds they made."

"Didn't you camp last night?" They'd had dinner Thursday night, like she'd agreed. And she'd stayed for devotions—vespers, he called it. He'd been unable to walk her home—something about an unwillingness to leave one of the campers unsupervised. "Did you get the problem child shipped off?"

"Yes and yes." Dave shook his head. "George. I'm going to keep praying for him. He has some bitterness and resentment already building up in his heart, and if he doesn't start making better decisions now, it's going to take a lot to turn things around."

"Would it have been better for him to stay?" She hadn't meant to ask—to seem like she was questioning his decisions. He was the one with a lifetime of mission work behind him, after all. He knew what would and wouldn't work. And yet, Elise knew a thing or two about needing love to soften a hard heart.

Dave ran a hand through his hair. "To be honest, I don't know. We might have been able to do some good for him. But he had the potential to do a lot of harm, too. He was already making moves on some of the women—and not all of those moves were rebuffed. This camp isn't going to become a place where single people hook up. It's just not."

"That makes sense. I—" Elise broke off when Joaquin stepped into the room.

"Everyone's here, and people are hungry." Joaquin smiled when conversations died off. "Let's say a quick prayer, then we can sing 'Happy Birthday' and get the party going."

"Birfday!" Leecey pulled on Joaquin's jeans. "Da. Up!"

Joaquin hoisted her onto his hip and kissed her nose. "Let's pray."

Elise bowed her head, but peered through her eyelashes to watch Indigo slip her hand into her husband's. Her kids were doing well. All of them. It was a good thing to know they were settled, following Jesus, and making families. Even if it also made her a little sad.

"Amen." Joaquin glanced at Indigo.

"What are you looking at me for? I don't sing." Indigo shook her head as she spoke.

Everyone chuckled.

Wayne started the song and everyone joined in.

Elise watched her granddaughter preen under the attention, then clap her hands madly when everyone finished. The girl was a doll baby, but also well on her way to being spoiled. Indigo wouldn't let it get out of hand. Probably.

"They're a beautiful family."

Dave's voice startled her. She'd been aware he was there—she seemed to always be hyper-alert when he was around—but for just a moment, she'd put thoughts of him from her mind. "They are. A rocky start that God redeemed."

Dave's eyebrows lifted.

"In addition to yesterday being Leecey's birthday, it's their one-year wedding anniversary."

"Ah. That'll make it easy to remember, at least."

Elise snickered. "So it will. Come on, let's get a plate. I don't think Maria's going to let Calvin finish beating me at Mario Kart until his blood sugar is back over a hundred."

"Is that what you were playing?"

Her cheeks heated. "Calvin knows it's the only game I have a chance of understanding. He enjoys it, too, though. So it works."

"I think it's nice. I don't know a lot of grandmas who would even try to play videogames with their grandchildren."

"How many grandmas do you know?" Elise took a plate and handed it to Dave before taking one for herself and starting down the buffet that had been set up on the long island where many of the more informal meals were consumed at the Hewitts'.

"Quite a few. But the majority of them live in a hut. Or a house that's up on stilts so if the Sepik River floods, their house doesn't." He smiled as he scooped food onto his plate. "That's in Papua New Guinea, in case you were wondering."

"I was. Although the country name doesn't actually help me overmuch. Is that in Africa somewhere?"

"No. It's part of Melanesia."

Elise glanced over her shoulder at him. "Is that supposed to tell me something?"

"Sorry. Pacific Ocean. North of Australia, east of Indonesia. But it's not Polynesia and it's not Micronesia."

"Okay." That seemed the safest answer. Polynesia, she sort of knew. Hawaii was Polynesian, wasn't it? If nothing else, relative to Australia gave her the general direction on the globe. "Do you miss it?"

Dave settled beside her on the couch and balanced his plate on his knees. "Yes and no. I still go two or three times a year. Not always to the same tribes where Mary and I worked—but I've taken on a sort of troubleshooter role in addition to these camps. So they send me out to help if there's an emergency with the career missionaries. But it's different than being there—and knowing you're going to stay—for years at a time. I work less with the people we're ministering to now, and more with the missionaries. It's different."

"I imagine the people you help are grateful you're there."

He smiled and scooped up some barbecue pork. "I hope so."

How was she supposed to respond to that? Maybe she wasn't. She focused on her plate instead.

"Thanks for letting me come to this party."

She glanced over, her eyebrows drawn together. It was on her lips to remind him she hadn't been the one to extend the invitation, but even in her head it sounded ungracious. She focused on making her lips curve up. "I'm glad you came."

He smiled at her. It did strange things to her insides. She shouldn't feel warm and tingly just because a man—and okay, her daughter was right, a *handsome* man—smiled at her.

But she did.

She just wasn't sure what, if anything, to do about it.

10

Dave stretched his arms up over his head and leaned back. Little cracks and pops came along with the motion. Signs of age. And probably an indication that sleeping on the ground wasn't as easy as it had been forty years ago. Still, based on the grumbles he heard coming from the rest of the shelters, he wasn't the only one feeling five nights of camping.

"We're going back to the lodge today, right Dave?" Missy, one of the ladies Dave considered best suited for the life of a missionary, groaned as she carried an armful of wood toward the firepit. "I need a shower."

"We'll head back after lunch, yes. You'll all get the afternoon and evening off. I talked with Mr. Hewitt on Saturday and he was going to arrange for some vans into town for anyone who wanted to see civilization."

There were ragged cheers throughout the camp. Dave smiled. Taos didn't seem like a place where they could get into too much trouble. And none of the remaining campers were liable to be looking for trouble, anyway.

After George had been sent home, Dave had two of the

women giving him the side-eye for a day, but they seemed to have gotten over it. One of them, he knew, had gone to see Elise on Sunday afternoon. Did he owe her thanks for setting them straight? Maybe he'd see if he could figure that out when they got back to the lodge.

He was looking forward to seeing her.

There had been a part of him—a large part of him—that hoped time away would settle his thoughts and get rid of whatever attraction he was feeling toward her. He'd done a lot of praying to that end, too. Now, the prospect of heading to the lodge and seeing Elise was going to make the morning drag. With the campers out of the way for the afternoon and evening, would he be able to convince her to spend time with him?

He wanted to ask her on a date.

Dave shook his head. Dating, at his age. He'd promised himself he wasn't going to be one of those men on the hunt for a newer, younger model. But here he was. And okay, fine, it wasn't as if Elise was in her twenties or thirties—she was perfectly age-appropriate for him. Seven years was no big deal once a couple hit their thirties.

Was she interested? Even the teeny, tiniest bit?

That was a question he didn't know how to answer.

So he'd just ask outright as soon as he had a moment to spare. But now was not the time. He looked around the camp. Everyone had started on their morning chores. At this point, they had the rhythm and routine down and made short work of getting breakfast going, tidying up the area to make it less appealing to wildlife, and still making time for prayer and Bible study.

Dave rolled up his bedroll and stuffed his other belongings into his backpack. He set the combination outside his lean-to so it was ready for the hike back to the lodge, then headed over to the campfire. "How can I help?"

"We've got it." Sarah nodded toward the coffee pot. "Get yourself a drink and take a seat. Thad and Sean should be ready to start serving soon."

"What are we having?" Dave filled a metal mug with coffee and sipped.

"Oatmeal." Sarah stirred the large black pot that hung over the fire.

Dave nodded. They'd brought staples out with them, so it made sense to allow their use. Their dinners had been whatever small animals they'd managed to snare in the traps they'd set up a little ways from the campsite. Rabbits. Squirrel. He smiled to himself. Not everyone had appreciated the reality of living off the land. He and Mary hadn't been particularly excited to choke down a bowlful of grubs their first night in a village, either. They'd done it, though, and lived to tell the tale.

Missionaries to more populated places had their own eating challenges. He and Mary had made friends with countless other couples who had tales of fish-eye soup and other local delicacies that the modern American stomach didn't consider edible.

When everyone had gathered and filled their cups and bowls, Dave said a short prayer for the meal.

"While you're eating, let's go over the schedule for today." He waited for the requisite groans. At this point, they were good natured, though they hadn't been the first few days. "We'll clean up from breakfast and then get the campsite ready for us to be gone for two days. That means it's crucially important that the fire is completely out—not just banked. I want someone to put their hand in those ashes. If there's any warmth at all, it needs more water on it."

Heads nodded. That was good. It wasn't desert here, but it was drier than Dave had expected. The last thing he wanted to do was start a forest fire.

"You'll need to take all your belongings back with you. It'll give you a chance to wash your blankets and pillowcases. But mostly, at the end of the day, you don't want a critter deciding it's their new home. We can leave the shelters set up—though we will take them down at the end of our time here next week. Once that's done, we're going to hike back toward the lodge with a stop at the obstacle course on the way."

This time the groans were more heartfelt.

Dave chuckled. "It's good for you."

"How?" Sarah crossed her arms. "I think it's dumb. I've never heard of anyone needing to climb a rope or come down a net ladder just to tell someone about Jesus."

"Maybe not, but it's a good test of attitude and teamwork." He kept his gaze fixed on her and didn't voice the end of his thought that she was failing both right now.

She blushed and looked away.

"All right, everyone, let's get going." Dave stood and carried his cup and bowl to the dishwashing station they'd set up. He could lead by example, if nothing else. And if the harder aspects of missionary life weren't right for some of them, that was okay. Cities needed Jesus, too.

The morning sped by. Was it the anticipation of getting to see Elise again? Dave didn't examine that stray thought too closely. Still, he was at the front of the pack heading down the path toward the lodge after they finished at the obstacle course.

He checked his watch. Just about two. They were more or less right on schedule.

Dave stopped at the base of the lodge steps and waited for everyone to make their way to him. "Great job, everyone. Head on inside, you all still have your room keys, right?"

Everyone nodded.

"Good. Grab showers, there's a big laundry room with multiple washers at the far end of the hall if you want to start some wash, or you can nap. The afternoon and evening are yours. There's no group dinner, either. I've arranged for some vans to carry people into town if you'd like to do a little sight-seeing and maybe grab a bite at a restaurant. The first of those should show up in a little over an hour. So you have time to shower first. Notice how often I'm suggesting showers?" Dave grinned when everyone chuckled. "The last van will leave from town to bring folks back to the lodge at a quarter after seven. We'll be having devotions at eight, and I expect to see everyone there. Questions?"

No one spoke.

Dave gestured toward the lodge. "Get on with it then. Enjoy your freedom."

The cheer that went up was a little weak—Dave apparently wasn't the only person who hadn't slept super well on the hard ground multiple nights in a row—but the group plodded past with a little more animated conversation than they'd managed before.

He brought up the rear and made sure to tug the door closed behind him. He could use a shower himself. He ought to head straight up. And yet. His gaze landed on Elise.

She was tucked in the corner of the main room, working the spinning wheel. The yarn was a dark blue this time. She must have finished the other. Of course, she had. They'd been gone several days.

Elise glanced up and smiled. "I wondered where you were."

"Have to make sure everyone else made it back." He wandered a little closer. Not too close—the shower conversation wasn't just for the campers. "How'd it go?"

"Good. I had a couple of visitors. They didn't run screaming or burst into tears, so I guess I did an okay job."

He laughed. "They said you were very helpful. Thank you."

"I'm glad." Elise stopped the wheel and folded her hands in

her lap. "It's not what I expected. Although, to be fair, I'm not sure what I expected."

"I feel like a lot of life is like that."

Elise chuckled. "That's true."

"I guess I'll head up. I want to get a shower before they use all the hot water."

"Of course. I overheard a few snippets of conversation when the group came through—you're going into town?"

"It's an option. Wayne arranged some vans. They have free time and Jillian won't be up to make dinner." He held her gaze. "Do you have dinner plans?"

"Me? Oh, I'll just go back to my cabin and fix something. Do you want me to wait here in case someone decides they'd like to chat instead of going into town?"

"Could I take you to dinner in town? As a thank you?"

"What are we doing, Dave?"

"Hopefully having dinner."

Her lips twitched.

Dave hitched his pack up on his shoulders to readjust it. "I'd like to get to know you better. Spend some time alone. I'm interested in you, and I can't say I ever thought I'd be in this position again, but I'd like to see where it goes."

"That's . . . blunt."

"I guess I don't see the point in beating around the bush. Is that wrong?" Should he have been more subtle? It wasn't his style—never had been—and even though he was here for two months, that was a short period of time when all was said and done.

"No. No, it's not wrong." Elise reached for her phone and clicked the screen on. "Why don't you come for dinner at my cabin? Say six?"

"Okay. I'm happy to take you out, though, if you don't want to cook."

She shook her head. "I don't mind. It won't be fancy, mind you."

"I don't need fancy. How will I know which cabin is yours?" There were a lot of cabins on that end of the property.

"You remember where the trail came out the first time we met?"

"Sure."

"I'm in that row. I'll come out on the porch at six."

"Okay." He glanced down. There were a lot of hours between now and six. And there was paperwork to do along with other chores. "I'll leave you to it and see you later."

Elise lifted her fingers in a little wave before starting the spinning wheel back up.

Dave headed toward the stairs, lining up the tasks he needed to get done in the order they should be tackled. Shower first, for sure. And then he could knock out the others as they came.

He was digging his key out of his pack when he felt a tap on his shoulder.

"Dave?"

He turned. "Hey, Jerome."

"Do you have a couple of minutes?" Jerome's Adam's apple bobbed nervously.

"Of course. Come on in. I'd like to set this pack down and unlace my boots." Dave was already mentally rearranging his schedule. Hopefully he could still make dinner—there should be plenty of time—but the mission came first. Always.

As he gestured for Jerome to sit, Dave prayed for wisdom and understanding. "What's up?"

11

"Smells good, Mom." Indigo dropped into one of the chairs at Elise's kitchen table. "What are you making?"

"Just some stir fry. Did you need something?" Elise cast a glance over her shoulder. Dave would be showing up in twenty minutes and she really didn't need her daughter here when that happened. She didn't want to explain what was going on. Especially since she didn't really understand it herself.

"No. Just thought I'd swing by and see how you're doing. Joaquin has Leecey at the stables—she's mad for Blaze these days. Sophie says she can start taking simple lessons whenever she wants. It seems too early, to me, but what do I know? Anyway, I miss having you around during the day, so I figured since I was on my own, I'd stop by."

"Oh. Thanks." Elise smiled and stirred the food. "I miss being in the shop. I miss seeing Leecey. And you, of course."

Indigo laughed. "Of course. That's a lot of food. Are you batch cooking now?"

Elise sighed. "No."

Indigo waited, then asked, "You're super hungry?"

Elise contemplated letting that stand as the answer, but she hadn't lied to her children when she was raising them, and she didn't want to start now. "No. Dave is coming over."

"Really?" Indigo squealed and clapped her hands together. "Why isn't the table set?"

Elise glanced over at the table and frowned. It was fine. There were placemats out and napkins in the holder in the center. She had salt and pepper shakers within easy reach. "I figured I'd serve at the stove. So we just need silverware."

"Oh, Mom." Indigo shook her head. "Come on. This isn't how you set the scene for romance."

"Well, good. I'm not trying to set the scene for that. It's just a friendly dinner." She'd been repeating that to herself since she'd invited him to come. She didn't have any expectations—refused to, in fact. "I'm just doing something nice for someone."

"I'm glad you're having him to dinner. I think you ought to take a little more care, though. Weren't you the one who always said it was our job, as a host, to ensure our guests felt welcome and treasured?"

Elise closed her eyes. It had only been a matter of time before her words got tossed in her face. To be honest, she was surprised it had taken this long. "That's different, and you know it."

"No, I don't." Indigo frowned at the table. "Where do you store your tablecloths?"

"I sold them all before I came here, remember?" Elise adjusted the fire under the pan. "This is what I have. If it's not good enough for him, then I guess it's just not good enough."

Indigo held up her hands. "Okay. The table can't be fixed. But you could go put on a dress. What about the one with the sunflowers on it?"

"What? No. I'm not dressing up." She certainly wasn't going to wear that dress. Elise wasn't quite sure how she'd come to own it in the first place. Skye and Indigo had ganged up on her when she'd been paging through a catalog. The next thing she'd known, she'd had a package arriving in a week. "I'm absolutely serious, Indigo. Friendly dinner. That's not sunflower sundress territory."

"Oh, come on. You look amazing in it."

"My arms—"

"Are fantastic. But if you're nervous about them, put that thin white sweater on, too." Indigo stood, pushed the chair in, and crossed to her mom. She put a hand on both her arms and held her gaze. "Dave is a great guy. You deserve to have someone in your life who can treasure you."

Elise shook her head. "Don't be ridiculous, I'm not—"

"Do it for me then? Please?"

Elise sighed. She'd never been able to hold out against Indigo when the girl got her stubborn on. "You're just like your father. You know that?"

"I do. At least in the stubborn department. I like to think I'm a little better off in other ways."

Elise kissed Indigo's cheek. "You are. But your dad wasn't a monster. He was just stubborn. And lost. And misguided."

"I didn't mean to make you sad."

"I'm not. Or not really." Elise frowned at the stove. The food was ready and would keep warm until Dave arrived. "The sunflowers? You really think?"

"I do. If you won't do it for Dave, do it for yourself. You have to admit you feel pretty when you wear it."

If she'd worn it more than ten minutes since it had arrived, she might admit it. Elise made a noncommittal sound.

"Go change. I'll keep an eye on the food." Indigo shooed at her.

"All right." This was a bad idea. The whole thing was. She could talk herself around dinner, but putting on a dress? That took it to a new level that just seemed like a bad plan. But it was too late now. Elise hurried to her room and slid the closet open. The sundress was easy to spot with its bright and happy yellow flowers. She shucked her jeans and t-shirt and slid on the dress. Even with the thick straps, Elise wasn't going to be able to handle bare arms. She dug through a dresser drawer until she found the tissue thin white sweater Indigo had made her and slipped it on.

It was better. She still looked like she was expecting romance. And now she needed lipstick. With a sigh, Elise went into the bathroom and applied pale pink color to her lips. That was it. She padded barefoot back out to the kitchen and stopped, smiling when she saw that Indigo had set the table with her nicer dishes and dug a candle out of one of the drawers. There was a note propped beside the spot where Elise usually sat. She picked it up.

Have fun, Mom. Let yourself dream a little.

She sighed and tucked the note into a drawer before she checked the time. Almost six.

She stepped out onto the porch and let the warm evening air surround her. What did Indigo mean, let herself dream? What was the point of dreams when reality was only going to keep getting in the way? She glanced over at Indigo's cabin. It looked empty. Her daughter had probably gone to join her husband and daughter at the stables. Or to collect them and go visit the sheep and alpacas.

Elise turned to look in the direction of the camp and her breath caught just a little as she saw Dave making his way down the path. What was she going to do about him? *Dream a little.*

"You make a picture." Dave offered a bunch of wildflowers. "I saw these along the way and they seemed to want to come with me."

Elise took them. The only one she knew was Indian paintbrush, but the bright red blooms were some of her favorites. But the flowers made her jittery—it was as if she wasn't the only one unable to remember this was just a friendly dinner. "Come on in. Dinner's ready. I know you have to get back in time for devotions."

She glanced over her shoulder to check that Dave was following as she stepped through the screen door. What would he see when he looked around her cabin? It wasn't anything out of a magazine. Most of what she had was what had been here when she came. It worked well enough for her needs. She'd added a few personal touches here and there, but the only decoration she really cared about was the large painting of sunset over the *Sangre de Cristo* Mountains that Azure had given her.

"I'll put these in some water. You can have a seat at the table." Elise went into the little kitchen and got down the cut glass vase she'd picked up at the church rummage sale. She filled it with water, dropped the wildflowers in, and turned—nearly ramming into Dave. "Oh."

"You have a lovely home."

Heat seared her cheeks. Why was he so close? "Thank you."

"I can take those, put them on the table for you." His fingers caressed hers as he wrapped his hand around the vase.

Her mouth was dry and blood pounded in her head. There was no way she'd be able to speak—and she couldn't organize the thoughts in her head well enough to get out something that wasn't lame, anyway—so she nodded.

His lips quirked up. "Am I making you nervous?"

She nodded again and managed to force a few words out. "A little."

"In a bad way?"

"No." Her voice was breathy. "Or, I guess, not really."

Dave reached around her and set the vase on the counter. He

stepped closer, invading her space fully, and slid his arms around her waist, holding her close.

Elise stiffened, then relaxed. How long had it been since someone had held her? Had Martin *ever* held her like this? She laid her head in the hollow of his shoulder and breathed in the mix of woodsy smells that were either his soap or aftershave. Maybe a combination of them? She circled him with her arms and let her eyes drift closed.

If she'd ever felt this safe, this cherished, before, she couldn't say when.

How long had they stood like that before his arms loosened? He brushed a kiss to her forehead, and stepped back.

Elise pressed her lips together and looked away. "Dinner's ready."

"How can I help?"

"Um." Where was her brain? Lost in that hug, that was where. Calling it a hug didn't seem to even scratch the surface— not when she lined it up next to any other hug she'd had in recent memory. Dinner. Right. "You can tell me what you'd like to drink, and I guess put those flowers on the table."

"Water always works, unless you have lemonade." He leaned past her—close enough that she caught another woodsy sniff— to get the vase.

She fought off a line of shivers that wanted to form on her spine. "I made some lemonade yesterday, actually."

"I can get it, if that's okay?" Dave pointed to the fridge.

"Of course. Thank you." Elise turned to the stove and made quick work of putting the meal onto the serving dishes Indigo had left out. She carried them over to the table and set them down before reaching for her chair. Dave beat her to it, sliding the chair out and holding it as she sat, then scooting it in. "Thanks. Again."

He chuckled and took his own seat. "It smells wonderful. So I guess it's my turn to say thank you."

Elise filled their glasses with lemonade.

Dave reached for her hand, his warm fingers curling around hers. "Can I say grace?"

"Of course." She bit off another thank you. It was awkward and ridiculous. She closed her eyes and bowed her head and tried to focus on anything other than her hand in his. With mixed results. She caught maybe every third word of his prayer. "Amen."

He gave her fingers a light squeeze before releasing them.

"It's just stir fry—so there's rice and then the chicken. I have more soy sauce if you want to add extra." She started to rise.

"I'm sure it's fine. You know, when I was in the field, Mary and I used to joke about how much we missed pasta. There's not a lot of that in the jungle, as you can probably imagine. But now? It's a staple at camps. And church receptions. And as much as I love it, I'm over it. So this is an amazing treat."

She smiled and scooped rice onto her plate. "I've never been a big fan of pasta. With five kids, it showed up on the menu a lot because it's cheap, easy, and filling. But once they started moving out, I shuffled it off. Martin would ask, now and then, but he didn't seem to miss it either."

Dave took a bite and made appreciative noises while he chewed. When he'd swallowed, he took a sip of lemonade and looked her way. "Tell me everything I need to know about Elise Hewitt."

Elise laughed. "You already know it. There's not all that much else to add."

"I don't believe that for a second."

She looked down at her food. It was entirely too easy to get lost in his eyes, and she wasn't a teenager on her first date. She needed to stop acting like one. She set her fork down. "Why don't you go first?"

Dave nodded. "I can do that. You forget I basically fundraise as part of my living. That means I'm good at talking a lot."

She laughed, unable to stop herself. "Then I expect your story to be entertaining as well as informative."

His eyes sparkled. "Challenge accepted."

12

D ave clapped as the last camper climbed over the top of the A-frame on the obstacle course and scrambled down the cargo net to join his team. He stopped the stopwatch and grinned. "Nice job, guys. All right, huddle up."

Everyone came over, forming a loose half-circle around where he stood. "This went a lot more smoothly. What do you think made the difference?"

They looked at each other, but no one spoke.

Dave sighed. "Still?"

Karla raised her hand.

"Go ahead."

"Well, um. I felt like we were doing better as a team—actually helping each other instead of everyone looking out for themselves. Like, I had a hard time on the rope, and Seth took the time to show me how to lock it between my feet, and now I can climb a rope."

Dave grinned. "Yes! That's exactly what I was looking for. So how can we extrapolate that to a lesson or a takeaway that applies to mission work?"

"Well." Sean raised his hand. "We're a team, right? None of

us would be sent out on our own—there'll always be people that we're working with. Even the local population. And if we're too busy focusing on doing our own thing and getting through, then we're ultimately going to fail."

Dave nodded. Sean had already shown himself to be a natural leader. It wasn't surprising that he'd had the brains to find this answer, either. "Anyone else?"

No one spoke.

"Okay. Sean's right on. The only thing I want to add to it is not to lose sight of who's running the team. It's not me. It's not your team leader. It's not even the mission agency. God's in charge. He's the first and most important teammate. I only saw one group of four take a minute to pray before they started the course. You're thinking of going onto the mission field full time. You want to tell others about Jesus while you work in their community—you're only going to succeed at that if you're deeply rooted in the Word and in constant prayer."

Heads nodded. A few turned away, clearly ashamed.

"The best thing? You can fix it starting right now. We're going to break into our roommate groups and go spend the next ninety minutes in prayer. Talk to each other. Find out how you can lift your teammate up. Pray aloud. Pray silently. Sit together in quiet and listen for the Holy Spirit to speak to you. Questions?"

Karla lifted her hand tentatively.

"Yes, Karla."

"Do you care where we go?"

"No. There's a lot of nature out here—find a place that's comfortable and go there. No one at the lodge, though. Let's keep it outside with a good bit of space between each pair. Anyone else?" Dave paused and looked around. "Okay, get going. I'll ring the dinner bell on the lodge porch when time's up."

He waited while everyone paired up and started off. He

breathed out and started back toward the lodge. He'd managed to keep his dinner with Elise in the back of his mind so he could focus on the campers and helping them see what they needed to do. But now?

Why hadn't he kissed her?

He'd thought about it. It had seemed like she was thinking about it, too. He'd held her instead, and it had almost been more intimate than a kiss.

Dave smiled, remembering her distracted reaction. Maybe skipping the kiss had been the right thing. He was moving fast, and that wasn't like him. Was the sense of urgency because he was only going to be here six more weeks? He'd been praying for and about Elise since they'd met on the path up the mountain. Something about her called to him.

So he'd keep praying.

And while he prayed, he'd spend as much time with her as she'd let him.

It wasn't a long walk back to the lodge. A few groups had settled on the grassy area near the front porch. It was nice to see them taking it seriously. Hopefully, there would be some good friendships that came out of their two weeks together, if nothing else.

He headed into the building. It wasn't hot outside, but he appreciated the cooler air inside. Dave glanced at the corner where Elise had set up the spinning wheel. It was empty.

He frowned even as his heart sank. He hadn't realized quite how much he'd been looking forward to seeing her until she wasn't there.

Dave wandered toward the kitchen. He'd grab a bottle of water and maybe a cookie. Would there be any of Skye's amazing cookies?

Elise spun when Dave came into the kitchen. "Oh. Hi. You're back."

He grinned. "Yeah. Everyone's out having some prayer time with the roommates before they head back. I've been looking forward to seeing you all day."

Elise's cheeks pinked.

He closed the distance between them and slipped his arms around her. "Was it just me?"

"No." She tipped her head up, and his gaze met hers. "I don't understand this."

"Do you need to?" He didn't understand either. Not really. But he'd also lived in uncertainty enough of his life that he was willing—and able—to roll with what God brought into his life.

"Seems like it would be easier." Her smile was weak and didn't reach her eyes. "I just—you're only here through the end of September. Then what? I'm not cut out for flings. And your job—I can't wrap my head around it. There's no space for me in something like that."

He managed a slow nod. Her points were valid. He couldn't say they weren't. It didn't mean he had to like them. "There's a lot in life that's uncertain."

"Oh, I know." Elise snorted. "I lived with a man, raised children with him, for years in uncertainty. I'd just as soon not start that all over again."

Lived with. Raised children with. She'd told him she and Martin weren't married, so why did it continue to give him a jolt? She'd been clear about being a new believer, but non-Christians got married all the time. It wasn't as if that was the property of the church. In the end, did it matter? "So . . . I should back off."

"I didn't say that." Her arms tightened around him. "I'm just —can we take things slow?"

"Of course, we can." He rubbed her back before stepping away. "Were you in here for a snack?"

"Skye said there were cookies. She makes these cherry chocolate chunk that are out of this world."

Dave nodded. "I had one Sunday. I was actually hoping there might be a few left."

"Well, if there are, I can't find them." Elise sighed. "I found a bag of store-bought chocolate chip, though. I could make some tea?"

"I won't say no to the tea." It wasn't his favorite, but he could deal. And he'd jump on any excuse to spend some more time with Elise. "I think they were over here on Sunday."

Dave moved down the row of cabinets and opened the one he thought he remembered Morgan standing in front of. The lower shelves were bowls and cups. Above them were canned goods and—*aha!* He reached up and wiggled a container out from behind some soup. "I think maybe these are they."

Elise finished filling the kettle and plugged it in before joining him by the island.

Dave pried up one corner of the container and breathed in the rich chocolate and cherry aroma. "Oh, yeah. She said these came from the back of a book?"

"That's what she tells me. I've been tempted to download it just to get the recipe."

"Skye won't share it?"

Elise shrugged. "She's been after me to read the series anyway. I think holding onto the recipe is her way to try and push me in that direction. But I just don't think solving murders is very relaxing."

Dave chuckled and lifted out a cookie. "Should we get a plate and be civilized?"

"Oh, probably." Elise turned to get a small plate from the cabinet and set it next to the cookie tin. "Is it wrong that I'd like two?"

"No. I was actually considering having three." Dave counted the cookies that were left and frowned. "Really, we ought to just finish them off. They're almost two weeks old. Won't they be getting stale?"

"I like the way you think." Elise laughed and loaded the remainder of the cookies onto the plate. "You're going to have to do most of the eating. I can handle two. Then I suspect I'm going to have to stop."

"We'll see how it goes." The kettle began to whistle. Elise pulled the plug and filled two mugs with hot water. "Do you want to choose a tea bag? They're in that drawer right in front of you."

He pulled out the drawer and considered the wide array of tea flavors. How was he supposed to know what went well with chocolate cherry cookies? He flipped through them with a slight frown. "I don't know what to choose. I like peppermint, but I don't think that's going to go well with the snack. I'd as soon not have caffeine, because I'm a man of a certain age and, sadly, that's started to impact my sleep."

Shaking her head and fighting a grin, Elise bumped him aside with her hip. She ran her finger over the tops of the packets before stopping and grabbing two. "Here. We'll do chamomile. It goes with everything."

Chamomile? Wasn't that the tea you drank when you couldn't sleep? He had a vague recollection of something that tasted . . . floral. He shrugged. He could roll with it. Maybe, if it was gross, he could conveniently forget about it and leave it untouched. That had worked with some of the less palatable local foods he'd been presented with. And if not? He'd choke it down. It couldn't be worse than grubs and insects.

"Why don't you carry the cookies, and I'll get our tea?" Dave took the mugs and nodded toward the exit. "We can take a seat in the lounge and have a little time before I have to call the crew back. Have you seen Jillian?"

"Not yet. I was a little surprised, actually. Then I thought tonight might be another night on their own."

He shook his head. Although, they could manage if it needed to become one. There were sandwich makings in there. That was good enough. "Should we worry, do you think?"

"No. She's reliable. If there's a problem, I'm sure she'll let someone know. Does she have your contact info?"

"I thought she did. I guess I can check my phone once we're settled." Dave looked around the lounge. Why was it so open? There weren't any cozy nooks for a couple to sneak off to for some romantic time alone. Which was probably on purpose given the general clientele of the camp, but it was frustrating now.

"Let's sit over by the wheel." Elise started in that direction. "It's a little more private."

Dave smiled. At least she had the same idea.

He waited for her to sit before handing her one of the mugs of tea. He dragged his chair closer and reached for her hand.

Elise twitched, then relaxed and curved her fingers around his.

She was nervy. Why did that appeal to him? In nearly every way she was the opposite of Mary. And maybe that was the best thing.

"So." Elise sipped her tea, watching him over the rim of the mug. "How did today go?"

He chuckled and felt the tension of the day drain away. The same as Mary or different, Elise was easy to be around. Comfortable. But definitely not boring. He didn't have to try very hard at all to imagine a lot of evenings that started out exactly like this one.

She was worried he was only here a little while.

Was she willing to be with him long term?

13

"Knock, knock!" Betsy's voice rang through Elise's cabin.

Elise smiled at the cheerful greeting. "Come in. I'm in the kitchen."

"Hi, hon. I just got back, and I couldn't wait to see you." Betsy dragged a chair away from the kitchen table and sank into it with a gusty sigh. "Why is airline travel so tiring? You're sitting the whole time. It ought to be relaxing."

"I've never thought hurtling through the air, thousands of miles above the ground, was restful. Your body knows it's unnatural."

Betsy chuckled. "I guess there's that. Can you sit for a minute?"

"Sure." Elise dried her hands on a dishtowel and paused to grab a box of crackers from one of the cupboards before joining Betsy at the small table. "Did you have a good time?"

"I did. I still wish you'd come with me. Azure missed you. She was trying to move heaven and earth to be able to come back with me."

"She has that big gallery show at the end of October. I can't imagine she's finished everything she needs for it."

"No. She hasn't. She said, and this should be a laugh for you, she never realized how challenging it was to be a mom and still have a life, because you made it look easy."

The words warmed her heart. It hadn't been easy, but it had always been worth it. Even with Martin and his unfaithful ways, Elise would never have traded the time she had with her kids. "Well. I'm sure she's doing better at it than she lets on."

"Oh, she is. This show is a big deal. I don't guess I realized it."

Elise nodded. She'd looked up the gallery online after Azure had mentioned it in one of their text conversations. "The man in Atlanta who gave her that first big break has been busy networking on her behalf. I'm sure it builds his reputation some as well, but that doesn't matter. Not when it's doing so much for Azure, Matt, and little Grace."

"Who's adorable and precocious."

Now she laughed. With Azure as her mother, Ainsley didn't really have any other options. "I'd hoped Matt might be a bit of a calming influence there. I guess he's busy with the garage."

"And his restoration sideline. Although he says he's getting to the point that he's going to have to make a choice between them. I imagine that will be difficult."

"Very. Although I think he'll probably find a way to make both work—either hand over the garage to a qualified manager so he can put his time into the restorations, or restrict that to a smaller number of cars and keep doing both. He strikes me as someone who's good at juggling."

"That's close to what Azure said. Matt reminds me of Martin as a young teen. He's the kind of man I always thought Martin would grow up to be." Betsy sighed. "I wish I understood what happened. Where we went wrong."

"It wasn't you. It was never you." Elise reached over and covered Betsy's hand with her own. "He made the choices. You gave him a solid foundation, and he walked away. He was proud of that."

Betsy frowned.

"When Azure told us she'd accepted Jesus, it was sort of funny to see him realize that our kids were doing to us what he'd done to you. Just in reverse. He would sometimes just shake his head and say parents could do their best, but ultimately, you had to trust you'd raised an independently thinking adult." Elise opened the box of crackers and fished out a couple. "I think the advice is good for you, too."

"It is." Betsy tipped the box so she could peer into it before pulling out a snack. "Did I miss anything here? I understand you've been counseling some of the camp women?"

Elise nodded but had a hard time meeting Betsy's gaze. "It's been interesting. And, thankfully, all stuff I'm qualified to talk about. No spiritual crises. Just homesickness, fatigue, and crushes on some of the guys."

"A lot like raising your daughters, then?"

"Close enough."

"Anything else going on?"

"I'm getting better at spinning. Indigo helped me bring the wheel over so I have something to do with my spare time. And there's a lot of it. I miss helping with Leecey, but apparently she's managing fine without me." That was good and bad all at the same time. Elise liked the idea of being useful—needed—but she was proud of her daughter for handling it.

Betsy sighed. "You're going to make me beg, aren't you?"

"I don't know what you're talking about." Oh, she did. But maybe if she played innocent, Betsy would let it go. Elise wasn't sure she was at the share-with-a-friend stage of things when it came to Dave. She didn't even know, not really, where she and Dave stood.

"Elise. If you don't want to talk to me about Dave, that's fine. I won't push. I'll just say he seems like a really nice man and a solid Christian, and I'd be thrilled if it ended up that he made you happy."

Elise's eyes filled. "I don't even know what that means. I loved Martin. For all his flaws—and there were plenty of them—I don't regret my years with him. Do I wish he'd been faithful to me? Of course, I do. But if I'd wanted him to be different, I could have pushed. I don't know if he would have chosen me if I did. And that eats at me. What if it's me? What if someone like Martin is all I have the right to ask for?"

"Elise Hewitt. How can you ask that?" Betsy crossed her arms, her expression stern. "Are you a child of God?"

Elise nodded.

"And are you a precious creation, made in His image?"

She nodded again, but didn't understand what one had to do with the other. "Neither of those changes—"

Betsy held up a hand. "I'm not finished."

"Sorry." Elise hunched her shoulders. It made sense, sort of, that Betsy could send her back to her teenage years. Back when her own mother had still tried to do something about the rebellion brewing in Elise's heart.

"Even before you were a Christian, you deserved better than my son offered you. I know you say you were okay with your agreement, and we don't need to go down that road other than for me to simply say I'm ashamed that my son asked it of you and sorry that you felt it was okay to accept. But now? God has a plan for your life. Maybe it's for you to be single and hang out here at the ranch. I'd love for that to be the case. Wayne and I both enjoy having you here and hope you'll always consider it home. But you're also young—and don't give me that look, you're middle-aged at best, which when you're staring down seventy-five is plenty young—and there are a lot of years in front of you, most likely. I'd love to know you had love and companionship and someone to treasure you the way Jesus treasures the Church. Because my son did a bad job of that while he was here, and I'll always regret it."

"His decisions aren't your responsibility." That answer she could provide. Maybe the rest of Betsy's tirade would need some time to percolate, but Martin had made his own choices. So had Elise, for that matter. She could have left. She could have insisted on so many things—marriage, fidelity, even settling down and getting out of the bus. There had been times here and there when she'd considered it. When another day handling five kids on her own in a school bus seemed like too much effort for very little reward. But in the end, Elise had made her choices, too. All in all, her life until now had shaped her and brought her to Hope Ranch and, more importantly, to Jesus. She wouldn't change anything if it meant those two items disappeared.

"I know that. It's still hard. You're a mother. You understand." Betsy reached for Elise's hand. "I love you, honey. I want so many wonderful things for you. Don't push them away because they're scary."

"Okay." Elise flipped her hand over and squeezed Betsy's fingers. "I love you, too. And I'm so grateful to you and Wayne. I want you to know that."

"We do." Betsy held Elise's gaze. "Trust me on that. Don't let gratitude keep you from stepping into the future, either."

Elise gave a wry chuckle. "You know me pretty well. I'll try."

"So. Dave?"

"I don't know. He makes me feel things that I'm not used to feeling. Things I thought were for young people, you know?"

Betsy's eyes sparkled. "I'd say that's a good thing."

"Maybe. I only have Martin as a yardstick. I felt all those

things with him in the beginning, and they don't guarantee happiness. Nothing does. I know that. But . . ."

"Is it okay if I pray for you?"

"Always." Elise smiled. "That's been one good thing about spinning yarn over in the lodge. It's quiet most of the time. No distractions. So I sit there and pray while the wheel spins, and maybe at some point I'll get some insight."

"Take some time to be still and listen, too. Sometimes it's easy to get caught up pouring your heart out to God, and we never hush enough to hear His answers."

What would those answers sound like? Just a quiet knowledge in her heart? Actual words? Something else? She could ask Betsy—she probably knew. Or would at least have some suggestions. But at some point, Elise had to start figuring her faith out on her own, didn't she?

So maybe, in addition to praying for guidance when it came to Dave, she'd ask God to help her know His voice.

"Can I ask you a question?"

Betsy's eyebrows lifted. "Of course."

Elise searched for the words she needed. "Dave leaves at the end of September. That's only three more camp sessions. Six weeks. Why am I even considering getting involved with him? It doesn't seem smart. At my age, should I bother with something that doesn't have long-term potential?"

"I can't answer that for you. I wish I could. It's certainly something to consider. Something to pray about. And to remember that as much as we love having you here on the ranch, you're not tied here. There's no reason you can't go where he is, if that's how things turn out. There are airplanes and cars and all manner of ways to stay in touch without being physically present—and that applies to you and Dave, or you and the people here at the ranch."

It wasn't the answer she wanted. Betsy wasn't going to tell

her what to do. Although she and Elise's daughters all seemed to be on the pro side of her dating Dave. So maybe they were telling her what to do. But there was a lot of difference between saying something was a good idea and figuring out just how that translated to the future.

Was that in itself the answer?

There was nothing stopping her from enjoying Dave while he was at the ranch and then letting it end naturally when he left. It would be a nice way to ease back into the dating world. No pressure. No promises. And a guaranteed end date, which in many ways made it safer.

She could have fun with an interesting, attractive man. There was no reason for her heart to get involved. And knowing he'd be gone in six weeks would ensure it.

Wouldn't it?

———

14

Dave waved as the van pulled out of the lodge parking lot carrying the last group of campers to the airport. They'd finished well. All of them. His reports were filed with the mission agency and he had the whole day ahead of him with nothing planned.

"They're gone?" Skye stepped out onto the porch with a mug cradled in her hands. "I'd planned to come see them off with you. It's kind of my job."

He chuckled and strode over to sit on the steps. "I don't think anyone minded. We haven't spent the kind of time in the camp area that most people probably do. I'm not sure half of them even realized you keep things running in the background."

"There's that. It's been almost like a vacation." Skye lowered herself to a step and leaned against the railing before taking a sip. "The next wave comes tomorrow?"

He nodded. "This group's smaller. Only six. Two married couples, two solo guys."

"Kids?"

"Nope. One of the couples is in their late forties and looking to retire early and do something meaningful with the last part of their life since they focused on careers and never made time for family. The others are young and just starting out. Should be interesting." He drummed his fingers on his knee. Was it showing his cards if he asked about Elise? Skye had to know he was interested in her mother, didn't she? "You don't happen to know what your mom's up to today, do you?"

"I imagine she's at the yarn shop with Indigo." Skye shrugged. "She likes to spend time with Leecey when she can. And Cara, when Maria's willing to let Mom babysit. Usually, Cyan keeps Calvin and Cara with him while he's working."

"How does he get anything done?" Dave couldn't imagine trying to do any sort of job with kids running around underfoot. The village children had all had tasks to do during the day. They worked alongside their parents from the moment they were old enough to help at all. The kids smaller than that were watched by the older tribe members so they weren't in the way. Since he and Mary had never been blessed with children, he'd never had to figure it out.

Skye laughed. "Cyan's good at multitasking. And Calvin's a good big brother. He doesn't usually mind playing with Cara—especially since she still takes two naps so he gets some good time to himself. But I think he's probably looking forward to school starting next week."

School. Right. "You begin in August here?"

"Yep. And although Calvin apparently made noises about being homeschooled when Cyan first showed up, he seems to enjoy public well enough. Especially now that he can manage his insulin pump on his own and doesn't have to visit the nurse constantly. Olivia should be back on Friday so she can start school also."

"Who's Olivia?"

"Sorry. She's Tommy's daughter from his first marriage. He got primary custody in the spring, so now Olivia goes to her mom's for vacation days. She's been in Japan since just before you came. I guess that's where Tommy's ex is going to be for a little while." Skye shrugged. "He's not sure. Anyway, Olivia's thirteen and so much fun to have around. I'm sure she'll be out to say hello. She's always curious about the folks at the camp."

"Your mom has four grandchildren?"

Skye's lips curved. "Five. My oldest sister, Azure, has one. They live in Virginia. She painted the mountains on Mom's wall in the living room."

"She's very talented." He'd noticed that painting. It had looked, at first, like a photograph. When he'd gotten closer to study it, he'd realized it wasn't. "Does she come out here to visit?"

"It's hard for her to get away. She has galleries that are always asking for her paintings. And her husband, Matt, owns and is the primary mechanic at a local garage. I wanted Mom to go out with Grandma, but I guess her staying was better for you."

"I definitely appreciated her help. The ladies who spent time with her said that she'd been just what they needed." He felt much the same way—Elise was just what he needed. Would he be able to convince her of that, though?

"Is your friend who broke her leg coming out?" Skye lifted her mug to drink again.

Margaret had emailed this morning. She could come. She was willing and cleared by her surgeon. But she wouldn't be able to move around well and the stairs to the sleeping rooms would be hard. "I'm not sure yet. There are some potential issues."

"I'm pretty sure Mom would be happy to keep helping out. She likes to feel useful."

"Everyone does." He smiled. "I don't get the feeling you'd mind if things between your mom and me turned into something more than friendship."

"No. I think it would be great. So do Indigo and Jade."

"Talking about us, are you?"

Skye shrugged, but her eyes twinkled. "Maybe a little."

"Well, I'm not opposed, but I think your mom might be. You might want to work on being a little more subtle." He smiled to soften his words, but he didn't want them scaring Elise off.

"You're probably right. I'd just really love to see Mom happy. She hasn't been for a long time. I don't think I realized that until this whole situation with Jade—do you know about that?"

He nodded. His hands clenched. The idea that any man would think it was a good thing to be able to mess around on the mother of his children still burned in his gut. He knew it wasn't uncommon—that it was, in many circles, considered progressive. He just thought it was stupid. "Your mom gave me the basics, I think, yes."

"Between that, and then Dad passing, and now? She's fine, you know, but she's not thriving. And I'm beginning to think she doesn't believe she deserves more than that."

"Deserve" was an interesting choice of words, but maybe it was better to leave that conversation alone. What did anyone deserve except eternal separation from God because of sin? And yet, God sent Jesus and made a way for salvation and restoration. No one deserved that, and yet in God's grace and mercy, it was there. Why would anyone cling to the idea that they deserved anything beyond that?

"I think, when you've lost your spouse, it's hard to imagine moving on from that." Dave took a deep breath and blew it out. It was still sometimes a struggle for him. "But I think I'll walk over to the yarn shop and see if I can convince your mom to spend the day with me. Any suggestions on what sort of activity would be tempting enough for her to give up granddaughter time?"

"There's a living history museum south of Santa Fe that she keeps talking about wanting to go see. It's a longish drive, but it's worth it. They have costumed interpreters showing the daily life on a Spanish ranch in the 1700s. Morgan and I have been. It's fascinating."

That could be fun. He liked the idea of a date that had a purpose. Wait. A date? Was he really going to call it that? He should. Hadn't that been what their dinner at her cabin was— their first date, to be exact. And the few instances they'd spent time talking and having a snack would definitely qualify as dates as well, if he wanted to be particular.

So, yes. This was a date.

If part of him that felt like he was being unfaithful to Mary, he'd just have to get over it.

"Okay. I'll see what she thinks. Do the online mapping services get you there?"

"Yeah. Click the link on their website." Skye lifted her mug in a toast. "Have fun. I'll be praying she agrees to go."

"You really don't mind? You're not worried about your dad and keeping his memory alive?"

Skye snorted, then her hand flew up to cover her nose and mouth. "Sorry. But no. Maybe if things had stayed the way they were before Royal and I did the DNA kit for one of his online video channels, it would be different. But finding out everything we did about Mom and Dad's relationship has changed things. It's definitely changed how I see my dad. How I think of him. I know it makes Mom sad, but I can't do much about that."

He nodded. "I'm sorry."

"Don't be." Skye shrugged. "Everyone has something, right?"

"Right." Dave stood and headed toward his car. He might as well drive over to the yarn shop, even if it meant going around to the front of the ranch and back. It would show he was serious about going—and maybe knowing he planned to go to the museum whether or not she came would make her more inclined to come along.

The drive was short, but full of beauty. The landscape here was unlike anything he'd encountered in other places around the globe. Oh, there were probably similarities with many different locales, but he hadn't had a picture in his mind of "northern New Mexico" before coming here. Or at least not an accurate one. It was lush and green—but not in the same way those words evoked. "High desert" was the term people used, but that left a lot to the imagination that his, at least, had been unable to conjure.

He parked in front of the yarn cabin and got out. There was a good bit of activity going on in this part of ranch. He'd driven past kids up on horses and spied Morgan working in the stable. There'd been someone in the pens with the alpacas, as well. The industry had made him smile.

Dave opened the cabin door and stepped inside. It was busy here, too. Indigo was spinning off-white wool. Elise was sorting vibrantly hued skeins of yarn into boxes that were arranged on the floor.

"Hello." Indigo's feet kept their steady pace on the pedal of her spinning wheel.

"Hi." Dave tucked his hands in his pockets. "You all look busy."

"It's not too bad. Getting a jump on some of the web orders that I want to take into town and mail tomorrow when I take Leecey down for her one-year wellness visit." Indigo glanced at her mom and raised her eyebrows.

Elise stopped what she was doing and stood, dusting off her hands. "Did you need something?"

"Mom." Indigo hissed under her breath.

Dave smothered a smile. She probably didn't mean for him to hear, but how could he not? "Just to see you. The lodge feels empty without you there."

"Oh." Elise's cheeks reddened. "I didn't think you needed me, so I thought—"

"Your time is your own. Although, since that's the case for me today, too, I was actually hoping you might want to join me on an adventure."

Elise's eyebrows lifted. "I'm not sure I'm up for any more snakes. I haven't been hiking, actually, since that unfortunate occurrence."

"I'm sorry to hear that. You looked like you enjoyed the activity."

Elise shrugged. "Not if I'm going to get a snakebite."

Dave laughed. "That's fair. Although, if we're being honest, I've lived through a couple. So they are survivable. Just not pleasant. At all."

Elise's jaw dropped.

Indigo stood abruptly. "I'm going to go check on the baby. I don't need those orders finished until tomorrow afternoon. You remember that, okay, Mom?"

"Please excuse my daughter." Elise shook her head. "She's convinced she's being helpful."

"I don't mind. At all." He reached out and took Elise's hand so he could give it a gentle squeeze. "Spend the day with me."

"I shouldn't . . . I don't—"

"Please, Elise." He waited until she looked up and met his gaze. "I'd rather not beg, but I will."

She swallowed and let out a breath. "How am I supposed to fight when you say things like that?"

He grinned and tugged her hand, drawing her closer. "Maybe you're not supposed to fight."

Elise closed her eyes. "All right. Where are we going?"

"Skye mentioned a living history museum that caught my interest." Probably better to try to keep that casual. If Elise wasn't happy with Indigo's interference, she probably wasn't going to get excited about the prospect of another of her daughters being in on it, too. "I'm going either way, but I'd enjoy some company."

"I've wanted to go there. They have a big fiber festival that Indigo is planning on next year. I'm more interested in the history—there's something about the Conquistadores."

"Is there?" Dave shook his head. Women had romantic notions about the strangest things. Plague. Lack of indoor plumbing. Hard, hard labor to survive? He'd had all of that in his lifetime in the jungle. He'd learned to deal with it. To enjoy aspects of it, even. But romanticize it? Nope. "I was thinking it'd be interesting to see how different it is from the way some of the tribes we lived with get along."

"Oh." She blinked. "I hadn't thought—but you've said that. It's still so strange. Let me check with Indigo. I know she said to go—but if she needs me, I really do feel like I've been shirking my responsibilities here."

"Okay." He dropped her hand and watched her disappear down the hallway. Did she want to go? Was she just being polite? Maybe the fact that he was only here for a little while should keep him from exploring a relationship with her. Except he was drawn to her, and he wasn't getting anything from God that suggested he should back away.

Elise returned, her lips pressed together. There was a little line between her eyebrows. "I'm not needed here."

Ouch. Maybe he should have a word with Skye and make sure the girls understood that they shouldn't make Elise feel unnecessary in their quest to push the two of them together. "I'm sure you are. She just doesn't want you to miss out on fun when it's offered."

"No. She said those words. I'm not necessary. She's been running her fiber business on her own since it started, and while she's happy to have my help, she doesn't need it." Elise snatched her pocketbook from behind the counter where the register and impulse buys were arranged. "Let's go."

Dave opened the door for her and kept his mouth closed. He didn't know what to say, anyway. The hurt was obvious—from Elise's words and her posture—so he started to pray quietly in his mind. He hurried ahead of her to grab the door to the passenger side of his vehicle.

"Thank you." Elise climbed into the car and slumped against the seatback.

Dave closed the door and went around to his side.

"I'm sorry." Elise pinched the bridge of her nose.

"It's okay to be hurt when someone says something hurtful." He reached over and rubbed her arm before fastening his seatbelt and starting the car. "I don't know a lot about the radio stations in this area. Or I have satellite radio. Would you like to choose some music?"

"Sure. Do you have a preference?"

Dave shook his head. "I like it all."

Elise studied him a moment before nodding and beginning to poke at the touch screen in the middle of the dash.

He opened a browser on his phone and searched out the museum before tapping the link for directions on their website. It was a decent drive—they should probably stop and get some food along the way. But they could cross that bridge, so to speak, when it was lunchtime.

Strains of the Beatles filled the car, and he laughed.

"Is this okay?" Elise clasped her hands together in her lap. "I could look for a Christian station, but I was in the mood for some classic rock."

"It's great. I told you I like it all. It's just not what I figured you'd choose."

Her eyebrows lifted. "Oh? What did you think I'd go for?"

"Classical, maybe? I'm not sure. Not the Beatles."

"To be fair, I chose classic rock. The station chose the Beatles. But I'm not going to complain."

He laughed and backed out of the parking spot, turning so they were headed to the front of the ranch and out. As he shifted into Drive, he joined in with the guys on the chorus.

He felt her staring for just a moment before she added her voice to his.

In many ways, it was just like the road trips he'd taken with Mary. She'd always sung along. In others? It was completely new.

Singing with Mary had always felt right. Singing with Elise felt right, too.

Elise looked up at the sound of footsteps. She smiled at Jade and set her book aside. "What brings you out this way?"

Jade set a mug of tea down in front of Elise and sat, cradling her own. "I haven't seen you in what feels like forever. It's weird going to lunch at the main house or dropping by the fiber cabin and not finding you there. So I figured I'd come and say hi."

"I'm sorry. I haven't been hiding." Elise reached for the tea and took a sip. She supposed her words weren't completely true. She had been hiding a little. There was no reason she couldn't head over to lunch with everyone—she'd just need to tell Dave so he knew not to let any of the women come during that hour —but things were awkward between her and Indigo right now, and she didn't want to get into it in front of everyone else. Nor did she want to have Betsy subtly prying for details about her relationship with Dave. The list could go on and on. "How are things with you?"

"Good. The VA work is picking up. Authors are already planning Christmas promos."

"Really? It's the first week of September."

"Right?" Jade laughed. "I get that there are details to see to, but it seems excessive. Whatever. It's work, and I'm enjoying it. Olivia's settling in at school, which is good. There were a few issues at the start of the year when a couple of the boys wanted to pick on the new girl."

"Oh, no." Elise set her mug down. "Is she okay?"

Jade nodded. "She set them straight right out of the gate. A little *too* forcefully. But it's all good now. She's made two new best friends who are, thankfully, also girls who go to church."

"Oh, that's nice. It lessens the complaining about that, I imagine."

"It does. She's still not sure about the whole Jesus thing, but Tommy and I are going to just keep on loving her and pointing her to Him and we'll take it from there."

"That's all you can do." Olivia might not be her grandchild by blood, but Elise loved that girl. "She's a smart young woman. I'll keep praying for God to knock down her objections. Her mother?"

Jade shrugged. "Still in Japan. Her lawyers got in touch with our lawyer to let us know that she wouldn't be around or available for the fall break, Thanksgiving, or Christmas but she definitely wants spring break."

"The less time she makes, the better."

"That was our feeling. Olivia doesn't mind. Or she doesn't seem to. Tommy's arranging for us all to talk with the pastor a little more just to keep on top of things."

"It's a good idea. Not one that I think would ever have entered my mind in that situation, but it's smart. I'm glad you found Tommy, honey, he's fantastic."

"Me, too." Jade sipped again, looking over the edge of the mug at Elise. "I'm pregnant."

"Are you?" Elise grinned and shot to her feet so she could

wrap Jade in a tight hug. She went back to sit, still beaming. "That's great news. How do you feel about it?"

"A little nervous, actually. What if—"

Elise held up her hand. "Don't do that to yourself. Right now, you focus on the baby growing inside you. You focus on your husband and your daughter. And if something happens, then you deal with it when it happens. Borrowing trouble is never a good plan."

Jade sighed. "That's what Tommy keeps saying. He's threatening to tattoo Matthew 6:34 on my arm."

"That might be a little extreme. The tattoo part. But maybe set it as your phone lock screen."

Jade blinked. "That's not a bad idea. Then I'd see it. Probably a lot."

Elise tapped her phone before angling it so Jade could see the verse she had there. She changed it periodically, when she was working on memorizing a new passage or needed a reminder that she wouldn't immediately dismiss. Right now it had 1 John 4:18. But maybe she ought to swap it out for the same passage as Jade—tomorrow did indeed have enough trouble of its own. And wasn't that what she was focused on?

"I love it. Thank you." Jade wrapped her hands around her mug but didn't drink. "You're the first person—well, other than Tommy—that I told. I haven't even said anything to Olivia. I'm nervous about her reaction."

"Because of how she reacted when her mom got pregnant?"

Jade nodded.

It wasn't the same. Would a thirteen-year-old recognize that, though? Maybe. Maybe not. "You should tell her before she finds out another way."

"I know. I was planning on telling her tonight. And then I figured it'd probably get to be common knowledge before I knew what happened. So I wanted to come by and tell you first. I know you're not my mom. Except in all the ways that count? You are."

Elise's eyes filled. "Oh, honey."

"Don't start crying." Jade wiped a tear off her cheek. "I can't keep the tears in no matter how I try."

"I was like that with Royal and Skye."

"Oh." Jade cleared her throat. "Twins. I can't—what if—"

Elise laughed, shaking her head. "It doesn't have to mean twins. But wouldn't that be fun?"

"For who?" Jade took a long drink of tea.

"Well, just remember you and I aren't genetically related. So if you're predisposed toward twins, it's not my fault. But I won't be surprised if one of my girls ends up with a set." In fact, she kind of hoped they did. Twins—once she'd gotten past the initial shock—had been a lot of fun. Hard work, yes, but all babies were. And for all his faults, once Martin realized that twins meant he had to help with a baby too, he'd stepped up more than he'd ever bothered before. "If that's what God gives you, He's going to get you through it. Think of all the help you have around here."

"That's true. We're already going to need a bigger cabin."

Elise nodded. She hadn't thought of that. "Are there any?"

"No. But Tommy was going to talk to Wayne about adding on. We like being close to everyone, and there's plenty of space."

"Or maybe, if you and Indigo swapped cabins, you could join my place with yours. I don't know. Expanding might still be easier."

"Where would you go?"

Elise waved it away. "I'm sure I could move back in with Wayne and Betsy."

"You're not planning on leaving, are you?"

She wasn't *planning* on it. Necessarily. "Let's just say I'm more open to the idea than I have been in the past."

"Because of Dave?"

"He's part of it. For sure. But also, you've all got your lives here, and that's wonderful. And, in fact, I'm not sure I need to be here to be a part of them. Look at Matt and Azure. I still talk to them—see them—several times a week. The video calling technology that used to be a far-fetched dream of science-fiction lovers has shrunk the world. I don't need to be here. And maybe I'm reaching a point where I'm starting to understand that I want to be somewhere I'm needed."

Jade reached out and clasped Elise's hand. "I need you here."

Elise shook her head. "I haven't made any plans."

"Skye and Indigo and Royal and Cyan need you, too."

Now she laughed. "The boys are so independent. As they should be. I see them so much less than I see anyone else. They're busy with their own lives, and since I raised them to be productive adults, I can hardly complain."

"But—"

Elise patted Jade's hand before drawing hers away. She hadn't given conscious thought to the idea of moving on. But maybe she should. Dave would leave in three and a half weeks. Would he ask her to come along? They weren't there, really. He hadn't even kissed her. Not a real kiss, at least. Her forehead? Sure. Cheek? Yes. And he could hug in the Olympics, if that was an event. And maybe it was time to live her life on her own terms rather than letting a man dictate them. "You don't need to worry about anything right now. Have you decided how you're going to tell Olivia you're expecting?"

For a moment, Jade looked like she was going to argue with the change in subject, then she sighed. "I got her a nightgown that says 'World's Best Big Sister' and then under it there's a babysitting rate chart."

Elise chuckled. "That sounds fun."

"I don't know. It might be lame. Thirteen is hard."

"Oh, I know. But this sounds exactly right. She probably wouldn't wear it to school, so making it something fun to sleep in gives her a chance to appreciate the humor without having to pretend to be too cool for it."

"You do know teenagers."

"I raised five of them. They're hard and wonderful all at the same time. And you're doing a beautiful job with it, especially since you were thrown into the deep end and didn't get to start out with diapers."

"I'm not sure that's an improvement." Jade chuckled, then sighed. "I hope you stay. We'd all be very sad if you weren't here."

Elise smiled. She wasn't convinced that was the case. And for the first time in . . . ever . . . she was going to figure out what she wanted to do. And then do it. She had her savings. She knew how to be thrifty. And she knew how to work hard. Surely there were jobs out there that she could do, even at her age. Even without a ton of experience and education.

She'd think on it.

And pray on it.

And see what happened next.

"I HEAR congratulations are in order, Grandma." Dave settled next to Elise on the couch and slid his arm around her shoulders.

Elise scooted closer. "News travels fast. And I'm not clear how it got to you when you were out camping."

"We ran into Tommy and Joaquin fixing a fence on the way to the obstacle course. Tommy mentioned it when I asked how he was doing."

Elise laughed. To say Tommy was excited was far too small

an understatement. Hopefully, it was easing Jade's worry. Olivia, from all accounts, was also pretty happy with the prospect. "That's good. He's a great dad. Jade's a great mom. I'm glad for them."

"And for you?"

She shrugged. "I guess? Grandchildren are lovely, but if it turns out some of my kids don't want or can't have them? It doesn't change how I feel about them."

"Nor should it. I guess I thought you'd be excited about another baby, since Indigo's daughter is getting older. Everyone says you're a genius with infants." He frowned a little as he watched her.

Elise looked down at her hands. "I do love babies. But I love toddlers, and elementary schoolers, and teenagers—you get the idea—too. There's always something interesting."

"What's wrong?"

"Why would anything be wrong?" She looked to the side to avoid his gaze.

"I don't know. You tell me."

Elise couldn't put her finger on the problem. Not exactly. But it all circled back to the idea of moving on, away from Hope Ranch. She couldn't get the idea out of her head, but she wasn't sure where to go. Or what to do about it. "There's nothing. I'm tired is all."

"I know that line." His lips quirked up at the corner. "It means stop asking. So I'll drop it, but I want you to know you can talk to me. I care about you, Elise."

"I know that." Her heart warmed a little. "I care about you, too."

"So what do you want to do tonight? All the campers are off on their own for the mid-camp break. I'd love to take you to dinner somewhere nice. We haven't had a fancy meal together."

"Oh. You don't have to do that." Her heart picked up. They'd gone on dates. They'd had quiet dates at home. A fancy meal, though? That felt important. Too important. She put her hand on her chest. "What if I fixed us something?"

"You do that for me a lot. And I appreciate it, but I'd really like to take you out tonight. Isn't there anywhere in town you enjoy eating?"

"Why don't we go down to The Cantina?" It wasn't a dressy place, but the food was good. It was a compromise, of sorts. She didn't feel like doing something formal. Or going out to eat, honestly. "Although we might run into some of the folks from camp. Would that be a problem?"

"I don't see why it would. I'm allowed to eat dinner, too. It's not fancy though, is it?"

She chuckled. "No. Do you really want that?"

"I want to do something nice for you. Something special." His lips brushed over her forehead, and she had to choke back a sigh. "I only have three weeks left."

"I know." She closed her eyes and breathed in the scent of him. She wasn't going to fall apart when he left. She was a strong, capable woman and was on her way to figuring out the rest of her life—one that didn't necessarily include Dave. Because they'd known each other for two months, or just about, and that was too short for forevers. At least it was for Elise. "I'm going to miss you."

"I'll miss you." Her head rose and fell with his sigh. "Let's not talk about that now. I don't want to poison these last three weeks with thoughts of leaving."

She could hold on to the illusion for a little while. But eventually—before those three weeks were over—Elise was going to have to make some decisions and let everyone know what they were. She'd start with a trip East to see Azure. The one she should have taken when Betsy offered at the start of August.

It would have been better for everyone if she had.

But she couldn't bring herself to truly regret meeting Dave. Getting to know him. Or falling for him.

Because no matter how carefully they avoided saying more than that they cared, Elise loved Dave.

And his leaving was going to tear her heart in two if she wasn't careful.

16

Dave leaned back on his pack and looked up at the stars. There wasn't much light pollution, and the Milky Way stretched across a portion of the sky. God was amazing. The last log crackled on the fire, adding a little heat and a little glow—more ambience than anything. The campers were all in their lean-tos, exhausted from a long day. This group was halfway through their time with him. They were the best so far. Everyone in the group enjoyed the outdoors and had camping experience, which cut down on the complaining about cooking out and staying in a tent.

His thoughts drifted to Elise. It was becoming more and more common for any spare time to bring her to the forefront of his mind. Something was off.

Their dinner on Wednesday had been delicious. And if he didn't think too hard—or analyze too deeply—their conversations and interactions had been much as they always were. But he'd been married long enough to know when a woman was stewing about something, and Elise was definitely stewing.

Maybe it wasn't his place to push. So he hadn't. Or not much. But she hadn't volunteered any information, either.

Was it because he was leaving soon?

There wasn't anything he could do about that right now. The mission board had emailed him about a couple in Brazil who needed relief so they could bring their daughter back to the States for emergency medical care. They were actually trying to get in touch with the campers for the last session and see if they were able to postpone—or if they could get Margaret and Herb to come run that session without him.

Dave had suggested sending them to Brazil, but Margaret couldn't do that long of a flight yet with her leg. They could get here—probably—but even that wasn't definite. Either way, it looked like he'd be leaving on Thursday instead of in three weeks, and there hadn't been any time to run back to the lodge to let Elise know.

Or not the right kind of time. He could have dashed down, told her, and left. He could call her—he had her number in his phone, and there was plenty of signal. But neither of those seemed like the right option.

Especially when she was already upset about something and unwilling to share.

He scrubbed his hands over his face. What was he supposed to do?

Rustling dragged his attention away from the stars and toward the shelters. Before long, William shimmied out of his lean-to and stood, stretching his arms over his head. He shuffled over to the campfire and lowered himself to one of the logs.

"Can't sleep?" Dave kept his voice low so they didn't wake anyone else.

"Not really." William picked up a stick and idly poked at the fire. "How do you know, for sure, that this is what God's calling you to do?"

"Prayer. Which I know sounds both glib and trite, but it isn't. What's troubling you about it?"

William's frown was visible in the flickering firelight. "I wouldn't say I'm troubled. It's just there's a girl."

As there should be when youth was involved. Dave smiled to himself. "And she's absolutely opposed?"

"Oh, no. She feels God calling her to missions, too. But she's drawn to the inner city. And I have this yearning for being overseas. Maybe the jungle. But anywhere, honestly. Just not here at home. I feel like it's too easy to get trapped in all the stuff here, you know?"

"I do." It had been amazing how quickly the tendrils of American culture had tried to worm their way into their lifestyle when he and Mary first moved back. Things they'd gone without for years were suddenly indispensable. "You know there are inner cities overseas, right?"

"I . . . hadn't thought of that."

"I happen to know there's an established ministry in Amsterdam that's looking to train a replacement couple. They're sort of a hostel-slash-shelter for teens and young adults who get trapped in drugs and sex work and don't know how to get out. Many of them don't—but they come back to this mission night after night for a clean place to sleep, a shower, a hot cup of coffee, and a listening ear."

"She'd love that." William drummed his fingers on his leg. "She didn't want to come do this camp because she's so set against anything that isn't in the city. She's so sure of her call. I'm sure that I want to marry her, but this disagreement has been making me wonder if maybe I'm supposed to get a normal job as a way to support her doing what she's called to do."

"That's always possible. What sort of career would you look for?"

William snorted. "Career? I don't know. Whatever would pay the bills. I've wanted to be a missionary since the seventh grade. Everything I did in college was focused on this. I have a degree in communications with a minor in Bible. It's not like that's going to land me an important, high paying job, but it might let me be a barista somewhere."

"You like to make foofoo coffee drinks?"

He shrugged. "Sure. I did that in high school for extra cash."

"Tell you what, I'll email the main office and let them know you might be interested in Amsterdam. Where's your girlfriend in the application process?"

"She's finished, same as me. She just really doesn't like camping. They didn't push."

"No. This is optional. And more for people who aren't sure about their preferences or call. Have the two of you talked marriage? Because I know they're hoping for a married couple to take over. Engaged might be enough."

"We've talked about it. A lot. I was on the verge of proposing when we started tripping over the city issue. Then I backed off a little—thinking maybe I was wrong about everything. But coming here hasn't given me that feeling at all. If anything, it's made me even more sure about marrying her and doing missions, but then I started thinking maybe that was a sign that I didn't know how to hear God in the first place. I started to question if I'd been wrong since middle school." William tossed the stick on the fire. "I wasn't happy about that prospect."

"I bet." Dave chuckled. "I'm glad you came out to talk to me. In fact, let me send that email now. They can get the ball rolling on their end to see if there's a fit. Maybe by the time you're on your way home on Wednesday, you'll have a better plan to talk to your girl about."

"Her name's Amber."

Dave nodded and pulled his phone from his pocket. He opened his email app and began to tap.

"Thanks, Dave."

He looked up from the screen and smiled. "You're welcome.

But this is why I'm here. Why don't you see if you can't grab a few more hours of sleep."

"Yeah. I'll do that. You should, too." William stood and dusted off the back of his pajama pants.

"I will." Dave watched William slide back into his tent before returning his attention to the email. When he'd finished, he skimmed through one more time to check the details, and then hit Send. He glanced back up at the stars.

God had set each star in its place. He knew when a single hair fell from Dave's head. He could work out what was going on between Dave and Elise—the same way He'd paved a path for William and Amber.

He'd just keep praying. And listening.

And maybe God would send some wise counsel along to help him out, too.

"I'm sorry. I wish we had better news."

Dave sighed and leaned against a tree trunk, the cell phone at his ear. "It's okay, Margaret. I figured it was a longer shot than the mission board knew. But a second surgery?"

"I guess the first one isn't healing like they'd hoped. The bones still aren't fusing. So they're going to take out the temporary hardware and put in something more permanent. Honestly, it all makes me queasy to think about, so I tuned out. Herb has the details if you want them."

"No. That's fine. Medicine was never my favorite aspect of anything we did." He'd done plenty of makeshift medicine in the field, but he'd never liked any of it. Just thinking about it had his stomach twisting. "I guess I'm queasy like you. So if you can't come, what's going to happen to the last camp session?"

"Herb was able to contact all the people who were registered.

No one seems overly upset to have it canceled, so that's what we'll do. The board is fine with it. You know they don't require the camps of anyone. It's just something nice they offer for the folks on the fence about signing on. Once someone commits, there's missionary school, which covers all of this and more."

Dave nodded. The camps had been his idea after the board had asked for suggestions to mitigate attrition from the six months of school. So he'd proposed these shorter experiences for folks on the fence—like a taste of what they might expect. And then, when he and Mary had ended up Stateside, it made sense for him to take them on. But if they still didn't see the value, maybe he was wasting his time.

"You still there, Dave?"

"Yeah. Sorry. Thinking."

"You're annoyed that they don't understand the value, right?"

He frowned. "It's not always comfortable having friends who understand you so well."

Margaret laughed. "It's a two-way street with you and us. And Mary was the worst—or best, I guess, depending on how you look at it—of the four of us."

"She was. She knew all of us so well." He sighed. "I guess since the board cleared the way, there's nothing to do but laundry and pack."

"That's the spirit. Of course, you're not hanging up yet."

"Why not? The crew has the camp basically broken down. We might as well get started on our hike back to the lodge so they can do their own laundry and packing."

"Tell me what else is bothering you, first."

He closed his eyes and counted slowly to ten. "I don't think—"

"Good. Don't think. Just talk."

He smiled. That was such a Margaret way to put things.

Mary always said Margaret was brassier than any doorknob. It wasn't always a compliment. "I met someone."

"Oh? Well, well. That's good."

"Is it?"

"Of course it is! David James Fitzgerald, you've been doing fine without Mary, I'll allow that, but you drift a little more every year. Tell me all about her."

"There's not time. I really do need to get this circus moving."

Margaret's heavy exhalation crackled in his ear. "Fine. Does she know you're in love with her?"

"No. Of course, I'm not. It's been six weeks. You don't fall in love in six weeks."

"Sure you do. How long were you and Mary friends before you proposed?"

"That's different. We were young and getting ready to head into the mission field. It was a different time."

"Uh-huh. Now you're old and getting ready to head into the mission field. And because it seems your memory has deserted you, I'll have you know it was two weeks. Two weeks between meeting Mary and a proposal."

"Why do you remember that?"

"Because Mary was my oldest and best friend, even then, and she had some serious concerns about the speed of your romance."

She had? That was news. She'd never let on—at least not in a way he'd picked up. "Did she regret it?"

"Never. Not for a moment." Margaret sighed. "Oh, boy, now I'm doubly annoyed at my clumsiness. I'd like to come out and meet this woman—measure her for myself."

"I think you'd like her." Maybe not right off the bat. Elise and Margaret were very different people. But in the long run, Dave was convinced the two of them would be friends. He needed that to be the case, anyway. He needed the two women he loved to like each other. Oh boy. He *was* in love with her.

"I'm sure we'd get along fine. We both love you."

"I just this minute realized I love her. I don't think you can say she feels the same when you've never met her."

"I don't think you'd fall for a woman who wasn't going to love you back. You're too smart for that. What does she think about you heading to Brazil?"

"She doesn't know yet. It's one of the things I need to handle back at the lodge."

"Why didn't you let her know as soon as you found out? You're just dropping this on her and then packing your bags?" Margaret muttered something that sounded suspiciously like "You're an idiot."

"I've been a little busy here doing my job. Remember that old thing?" Dave groaned. "I didn't want to jog back to the lodge and dump it on her when I had to hurry back out to the camp-site. That didn't seem wise."

"Oh, sure, it's much better to dump it on her and then leave the country." Margaret's voice dripped sarcasm.

Dave bristled. "I have a job to do. One I take seriously. I would've thought you'd understand that."

"Sure I do. I also understand no woman wants this to be the situation she finds herself in."

"Which is why I've never looked at anyone twice since Mary died." He swallowed and took a deep, cleansing breath. The campers were all milling around, trying to appear nonchalant, but failing. "Look. Everyone's ready to go here, so I'm going to hang up and start the hike back. Pray for me, would you?"

"You know I will. And for her, too. I think she might need it more. What's her name?"

"Elise." He sighed. "Her name's Elise, and she's wonderful."

"Aw." Margaret's voice softened. "I'll be praying she understands. Be gentle with her, Dave. If she's not used to missionaries, this is going to be a hard knock."

"Yeah, I know." He ended the call. Mary had been one of a kind. He was so grateful he'd had her in his life. Maybe he was doing Elise a disservice by wanting to keep things going between them somehow. Maybe he was being greedy. "All right. Everyone grab your packs and let's head back to the lodge. Who stuck their hand in the campfire ashes?"

William raised his sooty hand with a grin.

"Great. Who was on trash patrol?" He nodded as Jane raised her hand then continued ticking through the final camping area checklist. They needed to leave the site as close to the same as they'd found it as they could. If everyone was being honest— and why wouldn't they be?—they were set. "Let's go."

The campers fell into step behind him as he started back to the lodge. He wrestled with words, trying to figure out exactly what he should say to Elise. How he could say it in a way that would make it hurt less.

He didn't want to leave her.

He certainly didn't want her to think he was ending things between them.

But what if she decided that was the best course of action, anyway? He'd never had a broken heart.

He didn't want to start now.

17

Elise paced the length of the porch that ran across the front of the lodge. She twisted her hands together as she walked.

Dave and his campers would be back soon. It was their last day—there was even a van leaving for the airport after supper this evening for people who had evening flights. Tomorrow, if things went the way they had for the other camp sessions, she and Dave would get to spend the entire day together.

And maybe Elise would find the words to talk about the future. It was too soon. But they didn't have the luxury of time. Dave's camps would be over in two weeks, and then he'd be off somewhere else, and she needed to know his plans. His thoughts. What he wanted.

Maybe she wasn't the only one second-guessing.

There was nothing wrong with saying they'd had a fun summer romance. Her lips twitched. That sounded old fashioned and young at the same time. But it was accurate.

He'd never kissed her.

Elise blinked back the tears that burned her eyes.

It didn't necessarily mean he found her unattractive. Or

unappealing. Or some other un-word that she didn't know how to quantify. Maybe he believed in saving kissing for marriage. Wasn't that something she'd heard mentioned somewhere? One of the women's groups, maybe? It wasn't in fashion like it had been at one point—and from where Elise stood, that was a good thing. She could get behind saving sex for marriage, though even that had taken a little study and prayer to understand God's intentions. But kissing? That was such a simple pleasure—how could it be wrong?

Still. She wouldn't judge him if that was his mindset. And it was nicer to think that was the case than any of the alternatives.

She glanced at the trail that led into the forest and squinted. She blew out a breath. Here they came.

She smiled and leaned against the rail to watch them arrive. Well, to watch Dave. She didn't even let her gaze flicker over to the rest of the group. He was tall and lanky and strode like he owned the land—an easy gait that didn't seem to care about rocks or ruts in the path. He just took it all, literally, in stride.

Dave glanced up and his eyes warmed when they landed on her.

Elise lifted a hand in greeting.

He stopped, raised one finger, and then turned to hold up his arms. "Everybody gather in."

The six campers huddled around Dave.

Dave's strong voice rose. "You all did a great job the last two weeks. I'm proud of you. Go on inside, find your rooms, take a shower, nap if you want. You're all adults and I expect you to handle getting your bags repacked the way you want them and making it to the van that'll get you to the airport in time. There's a sheet posted in the upstairs hallway with those times, so you can compare to your tickets. It's been my pleasure to get to know all of you, and I hope you'll reach out if you ever need something. Go on now."

Elise chuckled. None of them seemed in a hurry to leave. Finally, they started toward the lodge.

"Dave?" One of the taller young men tapped Dave's arm. "Did you hear anything back about Amsterdam? I was going to give Amber a call, and I thought . . ."

"You know what? Let me check my email—I saw something from them, but I hadn't opened it because I got distracted." Dave glanced up and smiled at Elise. "Sorry. I'll just be another minute."

"Take your time." She wasn't in a rush, especially as she still hadn't figured out exactly how to say what she wanted to. Beyond all that, it was interesting to see him doing his job. She'd attended devotion and prayer time—he was a gifted Bible study leader—but it was interesting to see the other sides of his personality.

"Here we are." Dave was holding his phone and scrolling slowly. He smiled and angled it so the other man could also see. "Looks like you're a go, if you get Amber on board. At least for the initial meet and greet and some planning conversations."

The other man grinned and seemed to spontaneously drag Dave into a tight hug. "That's great. It's perfect. I know she's going to love the idea."

"Hope so." Dave patted the guy's back before easing away. "Go on in and call her. Let me know, okay? I'll be praying for things to go smoothly."

"Will do!" The man loped up the steps and into the lodge.

Dave turned slowly, tucking his hands into the pockets of his jeans. He looked up and held her gaze, his lips curving up. "Hi."

"Hi back. Everything go okay?" Nerves fluttered in her belly like butterflies.

"Mostly. And I think I might have helped William find a posting that'll work as a compromise with the young woman he's hoping to marry."

"Is she here?"

Dave shook his head. "She's set on inner city."

"Ah." That couple was a lot like her and Dave, just younger. "Sometimes people can't figure out a way to mesh their lives in a way that works for both of them."

"I think if they're meant to be together, they can. If they're seeking God's will and both are willing to bend to get there." He sighed. "You don't just mean William and Amber, do you?"

"I . . . no. You're leaving in another two weeks and I spent the last thirty-five years living for the man I loved, despite it not being what I wanted. Or needed. I can't do it again. I deserve not to have to."

"I don't disagree, but I guess I also don't think that's what I'm asking you to do."

"What are you asking me to do?" She looked away. He hadn't asked anything of her. They'd both avoided it—stopping with a mention of how short their time together was. "You leave and what, Dave? We write letters?"

He chuckled. "Well, I was thinking we could video chat and text, but I'm never opposed to actual mail, either. It just takes a long time to get overseas."

Her stomach dropped. "So you're not just leaving. You're heading abroad."

"It's what I do." He held out his hands as if imploring her to understand. "And I'm actually supposed to fly out tomorrow."

"Tomorrow. But the other camp session—"

"Got cancelled. The board wasn't able to find a replacement for me, and they need me, either way, in Brazil."

She nodded and drew in a long, shuddering breath. "Okay. I guess it's good I was going to try and convince you to let me cook for you tonight."

He closed his eyes, pain flashing through his features. "I have to go tonight. Since my flight is early tomorrow and only three of the campers were planning to take the van this evening, the board figured it was more cost effective for them to ride with me."

"I see." What was that buzzing in her ears? Her eye burned. "How long have you known?"

"Since Thursday."

Elise pressed her lips together. She wanted to yell, but what was the point? Hadn't he just made his position on their relationship clear? They didn't have one. She was a convenient, fun distraction for while he was here in New Mexico. And now, at least, instead of being angry that he hadn't kissed her, she could be relieved. Or that was what she was going to tell herself. "I'll let you get going, then. I imagine you have quite a lot you need to do before you go."

"Elise."

She held up a hand and backed away. "Don't. Please, don't. Let's just end this like reasonable adults."

"I don't want to end things. I want us to video chat and text every day. I want to know I'll be welcome back here in two months when I'm able to schedule some time off and we can see where this is going. I want you in my life. I believe God brought us together for a reason, Elise. I love you."

Tears left hot trails on her cheeks. She brushed them away and shook her head. "I won't be here in two months."

"Where will you go?"

"I don't know yet. I have some ideas. I guess we'll see what we see."

"I can come to you. Wherever you are, I'll come back."

Her heart cracked in two. Wasn't it strange that it felt possible? Martin had done such a thorough job breaking it before, she hadn't expected it to be possible to hurt this much again. "I don't think that's a good idea."

"I'll call you."

"That's not a good idea, either. You know it." Why wouldn't he make this easier on both of them? "It's better to quit while we're ahead. You have a life a lot like Martin did—full of travel and adventure. And I'm not content to sit at home and wait for someone to have time for me anymore. We're not compatible. And as much as I enjoyed our time together, I'm not going to settle again. If there's love in my future, it's going to have to be with someone who's willing to put me first. I don't think that's ever going to be you."

Dave frowned and shoved his hands back in his pockets. "How can I change your mind if you won't let me?"

Elise took a deep breath and blew it out before forcing her lips into some semblance of a smile. "Goodbye, Dave. Have a safe trip."

She slipped past him, careful to avoid any contact, and hurried down the steps from the porch. She wanted to run, but forced herself to take fast, measured strides as she made her way to the path that would lead her home.

She swiped at the tears that ran down her face, but let them come. It was time—maybe past time—that she let herself grieve all the ways she'd lost when it came to love. First with Martin. Now with Dave.

Well, there wouldn't be a third time.

She was going to make herself a life that didn't depend on anyone else.

And if she never risked her heart again, she could at least avoid breaking it a third time, too.

"I'M STILL NOT sure this is the right move, Mom." Indigo closed the station wagon tailgate and planted her hands on her hips.

"That's all right. I am." Elise peeked in the window and

nodded at her luggage situated beside the spinning wheel she'd purchased from Indigo. There was a tub of fleece to spin and they'd worked out a system for Indigo to ship new spinning orders to Elise as they came in. "I haven't seen Azure and Matt since the wedding. I have a grandbaby I'd like to meet in person for the first time. And while I don't expect you to understand, I could use a change of scene."

"I do understand." Indigo pulled her into a tight hug and held on. "Maybe it's because I understand that I'm worried."

"Well, don't be." Elise kissed her daughter's cheek and stepped back. "I can take care of myself—I took care of you all growing up, if you recall."

"You had Dad . . . and okay, you didn't always have Dad." Indigo's eyes filled. "What if we need you?"

"Then you'll let me know, and I'll try to come back. Or, you can hop on a plane and come to me."

"At Azure's."

Elise cocked her head to the side. "For now."

"What? Mom—"

"Stop. I'll be there for two weeks for sure. After that, I don't know. For all that your father and I lived in a bus, there's still a lot of the world I haven't seen. I might decide to go see some of it."

"The spinning?"

"I'll get the orders done. Don't sweat that. We're business partners and I won't let you down. But you know as well as anyone that I can do this part anywhere."

Indigo sighed. "I don't like it. I don't understand what happened between you and Dave."

"No, you don't. Because it's not your business."

"But, Mom."

"Indigo. Am I senile?"

Indigo shook her head.

"Somehow mentally incompetent?"

"No. You know you're not."

"Then stop worrying about me and treating me like I am." Elise smiled to gentle the words. "I appreciate your concern. I appreciate that you were appointed the spokesperson for your siblings so you didn't all gang up on me with your nagging. But the fact is, I'm going to be fine. Between my savings and the spinning, I can make this work. And I find I need to do that. You'd understand needing to prove something to yourself."

"Fine. But we're going to be praying that God brings you home to the ranch. Because this is dumb. And I don't like that some guy chased you away from your home."

Elise laughed. "Oh, honey. It wasn't Dave—not all of it. Don't blame him. Promise me."

"You're sure?" Indigo reached out and grabbed Elise's hand. "I don't like this."

"I guess that's turnabout then, as I wasn't thrilled when you took off with Wingfeather at nineteen."

Indigo winced.

"Exactly. But now you have Joaquin and Leecey."

"And a sibling of some sort due in July."

Elise grinned. "Really?"

Indigo nodded. "Just took a test today."

"That's great news. I'll be back to meet the baby for sure."

"Will you come for Jade's baby, too?"

"I'm not sure. Not because it's Jade, but because I can't be there at the drop of a hat for every baby that comes. You're all adults with your own lives, and I love that you want to include me in them. I promise you I understand how special that is. But I think it's time for me to spread my wings a little, too." Elise wasn't sure if that explained it or not. It made sense in her head —sort of. There was part of her that just wanted to unpack everything, go into her cabin, lock the door, and never come out again. Hope Ranch was as much a home as any she'd ever had, and leaving it was terrifying.

"I love you, Mom. Maybe I don't say that enough, but I want you to know it's true."

"Oh, honey, I know that. I know all of you love me. This isn't about that, or about you. It's about me. I'm going to be okay. I promise. And if I'm not? Then the first place I'm going to come is right back here to be with you all." That much was true. No matter what happened, she knew she'd have a place here. Betsy and Wayne had said as much to her last night. They were disappointed, too, though it seemed as if they understood maybe a little better than her children. "Now, I'm going to get on the road so I can make it a good eight hours before I stop for the night."

"And you'll call me when you're settled in a hotel?"

"I'll text you, worrywart." Elise leaned in and kissed Indigo's cheek. "I'll make a big group text with everyone on it and just text you all at once, okay?"

"If that's the best I can get, then yes. That's okay. Be safe, Mom. Be happy."

Elise nodded and pulled open the driver's side door. Safe, for sure. She wasn't as certain about happy—but there was some part of her that knew this trip was what God was telling her to do. Why? That wasn't clear. But she was going to step out in obedience and see where it took her.

18

Dave hitched his backpack higher on his shoulder and trudged up the jet way to the airport terminal. Weariness had settled in his bones over the last week, and now every step took extra effort. At least the board had found a full-time replacement for the Brazil situation after only four weeks instead of the eight to ten they'd told him the day after he'd left Hope Ranch.

He sighed and prayed for Elise, wherever she was. It was the only thing he could do. She didn't even look at his texts, nor was she answering his attempts to call. Maybe she'd blocked him or maybe she was just ignoring him. It didn't matter, really, when the result was the same.

He made his way to the baggage claim and then through customs on autopilot. He'd grab a taxi out to the house he and Mary had purchased and call it a night. At least he didn't have to worry about his car. The board had arranged to have it driven back for him, so it should be waiting at home. Maybe a good long sleep would fix the things that ailed him.

Hopefully the woman who managed the VRBO listings for the place had followed his instructions and it was empty and clean. He didn't have it in him to deal with one more snag after a day of international travel.

"Dave!"

He shook his head. People needed to learn not to holler like that in public places. There were probably sixteen men named Dave in the crowded hall to the parking lots.

"Dave Fitzgerald!"

Well, that narrowed it some. He slowed and looked up, scanning the crowd. His eyebrows drew together. "Margaret?"

She waved vigorously before clumping toward him on crutches. "Surprise!"

He reached out to give her a light hug. "It is."

"Herb's circling." She shook her head, her eyes rolling up. "That man's too cheap for his own good. I think it might have been five whole dollars for us to park and both come in."

He chuckled in spite of himself. That was Herb. It had come in handy many times, though. The man could stretch a dollar— or whatever the local currency was, even if it was banana leaves —until it begged for mercy.

"What are you doing here?"

"Waiting for you, obviously."

"You know that's not what I meant."

"I do. But let's wait until you're home to get into it. The nice woman who rents your house out for you got us settled yesterday afternoon. I've got a crockpot full of broccoli cheddar soup going and Herb made his brown bread this morning."

His stomach rumbled. Margaret was a great cook, when she put her mind to it. And Herb could have made a living baking bread. "All right. Lead the way."

"Welcome home."

He nodded and followed behind as Margaret blazed a trail through the crowd. Her crutches didn't seem to inconvenience her at all. It shouldn't surprise him. She was someone who always made the best of things, and if they'd told her she had to use crutches, she'd obviously figured out how to make that work for her. It didn't explain why they were here.

But he was grateful.

Mid-October in Florida was warm and balmy. At least it wasn't the summer temperatures that Mary had loved but he'd hated. Older people were supposed to crave the heat, but he didn't. Dave watched the cars that passed on the busy airport pickup road. "What sort of car did you rent?"

"Oh, you know Herb. He's always wanted to try one of those enormous SUVs, so he sweet talked the rental lady into one for the same price as a full size." Margaret laughed, her head shaking. "Some days, I feel like bargaining was the only skill he picked up during our years on the mission field, and I'm not sure I'm completely in support of that."

Dave grinned. "He was always the master. It came in handy, you have to admit."

"I might. But not where he can hear me. It's mortifying now that we're back in the States."

He could kind of see that. The US wasn't really built on the idea that prices were negotiable. There were places, of course, where it was less frowned on. Car rental kiosks were not generally in that group.

"Oh, here he is." Margaret raised an arm above her head and waved it.

A huge black SUV glided to the curb in front of them. The window rolled down and Herb's elfin face leaned toward them with a mighty grin. "Heya, Dave. This beast is amazing. Climb in."

"You go on ahead and get settled, Margaret." Dave wheeled his luggage toward the back of the monstrosity. The tailgate began to lift of its own accord. Dave raised his eyebrows. Fancy. He tucked his bags in the massive trunk and eyed the bottom of the hatch. There had to be a button to close it, didn't there?

"I've got it." Herb hollered from the front and a beep began.

Dave stepped out of the way and moved toward the back-seat door.

Margaret waved him toward the passenger seat. "You sit up front. I like it here. More room for my gimpy leg."

He started to object, but she was already settled. Her injured leg was up on the seat and her crutches were neatly tucked where they wouldn't be in the way. "Okay. Thanks."

Dave climbed in and reached for his seatbelt.

"Good surprise or bad surprise?" Herb glanced over at Dave before checking the traffic and pulling away from the curb.

"Good. Definitely good." Dave sighed and settled back into the buttery leather seat. "I didn't realize how much I missed seeing your faces."

Herb's gaze flicked up to the rearview mirror.

"All right. You win." Margaret chuckled. "I spent entirely too much time trying to talk him out of this plan."

"I'm glad you failed. And I appreciate both of you—Herb for insisting and Margaret for thinking better of it." It was good to have friends who loved him. And who understood him. Because Margaret wasn't necessarily wrong. There was a part of him—a big one—that had been craving the solitude of his Florida house. Except, he'd wallow. Even knowing that was what he'd been planning on doing didn't change the fact that part of him resented missing out on the opportunity to do it.

"You miss her." Margaret's comment was definitely a statement, not a question.

Dave answered anyway. "I do. I shouldn't."

"Pish posh." Herb frowned over at him before returning his attention to the road ahead. "Why shouldn't you miss her? We haven't met the lady, but from the little you told us, she sounds perfect for you."

She had seemed perfect, and maybe that was why it hurt—because it definitely hurt—that she was able to walk away and end things between them so easily. Dave shrugged and tried to sound philosophical. "I thought so too, but all the evidence points to the fact that she didn't feel the same."

Margaret snorted from the back seat.

"What's that supposed to mean?" Dave twisted so he could look at his friend. "Did I miss something?"

"How about the fact that she's in love with you?" Margaret pointed at him. "You have to admit you're dense about these things."

Dave bristled. "No, I don't. And I also don't think she was. She cared for me—her words, by the way—but it was obviously more like how you care about a sad puppy than anything else. And then, when something comes up and you realize the puppy isn't your responsibility, you walk away without looking back."

"Oh, Dave. You're not a sad puppy." Margaret patted his shoulder. "And you can't be sure she didn't look back."

An argument danced on the tip of his tongue, but he swallowed it. There was no point. Just like Mary, once Margaret made up her mind, it was set. Herb could, sometimes, get around her, but Dave wasn't going to make any headway there. He grunted and turned to look out the window.

Palm trees on the side of the road flashed by as they sped down the freeway. His house wasn't too far from the airport, but it was enough of a drive that he could lean back and let his eyes drift shut.

Herb must have turned on the radio, because quiet worship music lulled him to sleep.

A closing car door jolted him awake.

Dave rubbed his eyes and straightened. He looked around

and peace settled on his shoulders. Home. At least such as it was. He pushed open the SUV's door and climbed out, taking a moment to stretch out the kinks. Herb and Margaret must have already gone in—so what door had awakened him?

"Sorry about that." Herb stepped out onto the porch, hands tucked in his pockets. "I thought closing the trunk manually would be quieter than the beeping when you use the button."

"It's fine. You didn't have to get my bags."

Herb laughed. "I know that. But Margaret told me to, so I did."

Dave chuckled. It was a running joke amongst the people who knew them that Margaret was in charge. People who knew the couple well knew it wasn't the truth—they had a picture-perfect marriage full of love and respect. They took good care of one another. The same kind of relationship he'd had with Mary. The kind of relationship he'd wanted to have with Elise.

"Come on, let's go walk on the beach. Margaret's taking a nap. She won't say it, but her leg aches and using the crutches is a literal pain." Herb jerked his head toward the path across the street that led from the house, through grassy dunes, to the ocean.

Dave fell into step beside his friend. "Thanks again for coming to get me."

"We're worried about you."

"You don't need to be. I'm fine." The response was automatic—had been for years. When Mary got sick and it was obvious that they'd have to return to the US, then when it became clear that she wasn't going to recover, being fine was easier than the truth. And no one really wanted the details anyway. Not here. In the jungle? Sure. The tribe members never asked how someone was unless they were invested in the answer—and in helping, if they could. But here, the words "how are you" were a sort of verbal spasm that were meant solely to convey that the person speaking them was acknowledging your existence.

"How well do I know you?" Herb stopped walking and turned to stare out at the ocean.

Dave sighed. "Too well."

Herb snorted out a laugh. "That's probably true. Same goes, though."

"Yeah, I guess." Dave watched the waves as they rolled toward the shore.

"I have to wonder why you're not fighting for her."

"It was pretty obvious she didn't want me to."

"Didn't want it or didn't expect you to want to?"

Dave frowned. That was a question. "Maybe both. I did try. She won't answer me. I don't blame her."

"Why not?"

"I don't have the kind of life she wants. The camps, heading out on short notice to help out all around the world? She doesn't want to be left at home—from what I can gather, her husband did that—left her to care for the kids while he chased work. And other women."

"Ah." Herb blew out a breath. "You could change that."

"How am I supposed to change what her husband did to her?"

"Don't be dense." Herb turned his head and pinned Dave with his gaze. "Your life. The life you could make with her. It's not like you have to keep working for the mission board."

"It's what I know." Little fingertips of panic scrabbled at his heart as it tried to climb into his throat. "It's all I've ever known."

Herb nodded. "That's true. But it's not all that is. You know that. Look at Margaret and me. We've adjusted just fine to civilian life."

"You help out at the camps."

"For you, Dave. Only for you. Fact is, if Margaret hadn't

broken her leg, we'd planned to tell you this was our last year. You know the board doesn't need the camps, right?"

Dave closed his eyes. That had been made clear. As had the fact that, while they appreciated his willingness to rush around to help out, they had other, younger people who wanted to do it. There were missionaries in their forties who wanted to return to the States and take on this sort of role, but because Dave was still active, he had first dibs. They expected him to decline. They wanted him to. Nobody needed him.

Not the mission board.

Not Mary, since she'd gone home to Jesus.

And not Elise.

Dave didn't usually feel his age, but suddenly the weight of being sixty settled on his shoulders. This was the time when most couples were settling into their empty-nest life—a second chance at adolescence, practically, but with more money to fund the fun things they wanted to do.

It was supposed to be a new beginning.

It felt like the beginning of the end.

19

T he knock on the door had Elise looking up from her spinning wheel. "Come in."

Azure poked her head through and grinned. "Hi, Mom. How's it going?"

"Good. I still chuckle a little to think I spend my days spinning in a stone tower."

Azure laughed. "Well, there's no requirement for you to turn straw into gold at least, and the spindle looks dull enough that if your finger hits it, you won't get pricked."

"All true." No fairy tales for Elise Hewitt. Not in this lifetime. Dave had seemed like he might turn out to be a handsome prince, but just like Martin, he'd remained a frog. Of course, having not kissed, maybe there was still a possibility?

No. She pushed that thought away and stood. He'd made his choice. Brazil—or wherever in the world they asked him to go— would always take precedence over her. And she was done being second place.

"What brings you out here? Slow day at the garage?"

"I'm taking a day off to hang out with my mom." Azure

glanced around the kitchen and eating area that made up the first floor of the tower suite at Peacock Hill. "Want me to fix us lunch?"

"Is it lunchtime already?" Elise wasn't hungry. That was a recurring theme these days. She forced food down when someone stopped by and suggested it. That happened often enough that she'd figured Azure had spoken to Deidre and the rest of the crew here. "Why don't we take a walk, first? I can stretch out the kinks and work up an appetite."

"Sure. The grounds are pretty and always worth walking. Fall in the mountains of southwestern Virginia is one of my favorites." Azure stepped through the door into the October morning sunshine.

Elise followed, tugging the door closed behind her. "Where's Little Bit?"

"Oh, Matt has her. She loves going to the garage with her daddy, and he uses it as an excuse to let her get dirty—says he's teaching her the ropes." Azure chuckled. "I think he just wants me to have a break."

"I'd be happy to watch her, you know that, right?"

"I do." Azure slung her arm around her mom's shoulders and started walking. "You've been here a while now."

Elise frowned. "Do I need to go? I'm taking up the tower—that's probably costing a lot. I can pay—"

"Mom, stop. No one is worried about the tower being booked. We're worried about you."

"I'm fine."

Azure snorted. "Sell it to someone who's buying."

"I *am*."

"No. You aren't. Stop that."

Elise held her tongue as they walked for several minutes. The leaves on the maples—she thought most of them had to be maples—were fiery reds and oranges. She blew out a breath as they passed the clearing where a bonfire ring was surrounded by well-worn logs. "Okay. I'm not. But I will be."

"Will you?" Azure glanced over, concern clouding her features. "Because I'm not seeing improvement. And talking to the rest of the family—"

"Oh, why would you do that?"

"Because we're all worried about you. You're our mom, in case you forgot that. Well, except Jade, but she loves you the same way, so she counts, too. They all seem to think this is a longstanding issue. Like pre-Dad's-dying."

Elise pinched the bridge of her nose. There were some things that she just didn't want to talk to her children about. Maybe she could deflect. "Your father was a difficult man to love."

"No question. And he betrayed you. Also no question. But life in Christ is supposed to bring joy."

"I have joy." Didn't she? "It's different than being happy all the time. You get that, don't you?"

"I don't want to argue semantics. That's not my thing—you'd be better off with Cyan for that. Maybe I should have him call you."

"Please don't." Elise smiled. "I love your brother, but he can get annoying."

Azure laughed. "I've been saying that my whole life. The point is, we're concerned. And we were all on board with this Dave fellow—it's why I was okay with Jade, Skye, and Indigo helping push the two of you together."

"Excuse me?" Elise stopped and gaped at her daughter. No, they didn't.

"Oh." Red washed over Azure's cheeks. "You didn't know."

"No, I didn't know."

Azure sighed and started walking again. "Let's keep going, and I'll tell you what I know. Which isn't much."

Elise shook her head and stomped along beside Azure. Of all the . . . "Was that the only reason he paid attention to me? Tell me the truth."

"Not according to them." Azure bit her lip. "Skye says he made it clear he was interested, but you were pushing him away, so they just kind of encouraged him to be persistent."

"And?"

"And nothing. That's what I know."

"That's not much."

"I did warn you." Azure shrugged. "I don't see what the big deal is. From all accounts, you and Dave—it's Dave, right?"

Elise nodded.

"The two of you are perfect for each other."

Elise had thought the same thing. Until she hadn't. "Other than the whole I'm-never-going-to-be-top-priority-for-him thing."

"You don't know that. He had an existing obligation. Did you give him any time to make new arrangements? To change his life to make room for you? Or did you write him off like a bad debt and run away?"

It didn't seem like a fair characterization. Elise opened her mouth to argue about it, and then changed her mind. That would just be another semantics game—and if she pushed that too much, Azure was bound to sic Cyan on her. That boy . . . well, man . . . had his father's ability to argue the paint off a wall.

She crossed her arms. "I have a right to want to come first in someone's heart."

"Actually, you don't. But I'll give you second."

"You know what I meant." Of course she wanted Dave—or anyone—to put Jesus first. Wasn't she trying to do that herself? Every day. Regardless of how hard it was.

"I just think you should stop measuring Dave up against Dad. They're not the same person. Even Dad wasn't the same person before he died as he was when I was little. People grow and change. Sometimes that's good. Sometimes it's not." Azure put her hands in the pockets of her brightly painted overalls. "And sometimes you just have to decide if you're going to grow and change along with them."

Elise glanced over. "Are you and Matt having problems?"

"No." Azure smiled. "Not any more than I think every married couple has. We disagree here and there, but we're working through it."

Elise bit her lip. "Can I help somehow?"

"It's just the garage and his restoration projects pulling him in different directions. Matt has an overdeveloped, in my mind, sense of obligation to his aunt and uncle. So he's always going to put the garage and their expectations over his wants and needs. Unless I can nudge him to shift here and there so everyone's happy."

"Does that happen?" It never had in her experience. Hadn't Elise spent her days with Martin doing what she could to make sure everyone was happy? If she'd done a better job of it, wouldn't he have stayed? Found a job locally—or moved them around even more often—and stayed away from other women?

"Matt's not Dad. And he'll figure it out. Like I said, we're doing okay—just working through some shifting priorities. It doesn't help that I'm expecting again, which puts pressure on him to provide, even though we could live comfortably enough on my art."

"Oh, honey. Congratulations." Elise stopped and held her arms open. Azure walked in for a quick, hard hug. "You might have started this whole conversation with that news, you know?"

Azure chuckled. "We aren't really telling anyone yet. Anna and Duncan just had another failed IVF—and it turns out it was their last. The doctors have said there's nothing else to try. We weren't planning this yet, so it's salt in the wound, you know?"

"You're a good friend." Elise sighed. Had she ever been that considerate? Maybe. It was hard to look back and have an honest evaluation. "Dave stopped texting two weeks ago."

"Because you didn't answer?"

Elise nodded. Probably not her finest moments.

"So you text him. Or, better yet, call him. Problems don't get solved in a communication vacuum."

"I know you're right, but I don't know what to say."

Azure bumped her mom with her hip and started walking again. "Start with 'hello' and see where it goes from there."

She could probably do that. Maybe.

Perhaps.

Her stomach tightened and it felt as though she'd swallowed an apple whole. She could start with "hello," but she knew an apology needed to follow shortly thereafter. Would he accept it, or would he give her back the same treatment she'd given him?

Was it better not to know?

She wanted to talk to Dave—missing him was a constant ache. But it was better than finding out he didn't want her, after all.

"THANKS so much for helping us with the Fall Festival this weekend." Deidre, the woman who owned Peacock Hill and had brought Azure there to do some artwork, smiled across the long dining room table at Elise.

"I'm pleased to be able to pitch in." Elise scooped more candy corn and dumped it into a goody bag before spinning it and wrapping a twist tie around to keep it closed. "You've done a wonderful job here. Azure showed me the 'before' photos on your website, and the photo documentary you did of the restoration."

Deidre beamed. "Thank you. It was a daunting project when I started, but I knew this was where God wanted me. And then there was Jeremiah."

Elise chuckled. Deidre's husband was as besotted with her as she was with him. All the couples at Peacock Hill seemed to be madly in love. Just like the couples at Hope Ranch. It had to be Jesus, didn't it? They all had Him as the foundation of their relationships, and it showed. Elise wanted that.

She wanted it with Dave.

But she still couldn't bring herself to reach out.

"Once you finish with the goody bags, do you think you could hang some bats in the foyer?" Deidre held up a bright purple bat on a string. It had a goofy, grinning face and the wings bounced up and down cheerily as it dangled.

"Those are adorable." And decidedly not scary. That was the theme with fall festivals, Elise was learning. Candy, fun games, and just a few of the traditional Halloween touches, but shifted into cartoony fun rather than fear. She liked it. "If there's a step ladder, then yes, absolutely."

"Yep. It's out there. As is the box of bats." Deidre chuckled. "Thanks. I need to zip down to check on Jeremiah, since he's running herd on the kids, and then I've got to scoot out to Anna and Duncan's cottage. Anna's not feeling well, and I wanted to take her some soup."

Elise nodded. Deidre didn't owe her any sort of explanation, but it was something she'd noticed everyone at Peacock Hill seemed to do. Maybe because the property was so large and spread out? At Hope Ranch, people just texted. Whatever. She'd do candy corn, and then she'd hang bats, and when she finished that, she'd find someone who looked busy and offer up her hands.

"If Vanessa and Topher show up—do you remember meeting them?"

Elise closed her eyes and sorted through all the people she'd met in her almost two months here. Two months—when she'd planned on two weeks. It was time to move on, wasn't it? "He's a caterer?"

Deidre nodded. "That's them. Vanessa's the flowers. Anyway, they know what they're doing, but if they need anything, have them give me a call. Or Claire should be in the business office."

"Got it." Elise dug the scoop into the candy corn and started on another bag. Deidre hurried off—the woman was a little bit of a perpetual motion machine—and Elise focused on her task.

The plan was never to be here two months. How had she let that happen? Sure, it was convenient to spin in one place—but the wheel was moveable, and as long as she had an address for Indigo to send new shipments, she didn't have to stay put in between.

Azure didn't need her here. Maybe she enjoyed having her mom close—and even that was up for debate, because Azure took time out of her schedule to swing by and spend time, which meant she wasn't doing things that needed doing—but she'd be all right when Elise left. That was good. It was exactly what she'd intended when she was raising her kids—to turn them into capable adults who could make their own way in the world.

It shouldn't leave her melancholy.

Except it felt as though she'd done a better job with her kids than she'd done with herself.

Elise reached the bottom of the candy corn, filled the final bag, and then stood. She'd hang the bats, and then, instead of looking for more work to do, she'd get on her computer and figure out where she wanted to head next.

Somewhere warm for the winter seemed like a good idea. Maybe near the ocean?

They'd lived on the California coast for a while when the kids were small. Maybe it was time she gave the Florida beaches a try.

20

Dave dug his toes in the sand and watched the ocean. It had become his morning ritual in the two weeks he'd been back in Florida to walk the beach and then stop and watch the waves for as long as it took for peace to settle in his heart. Some days it went faster than others.

"Hello, neighbor." The hearty voice belonged to the man who owned the house next door to Dave's. The guy was probably in his forties and he had all the charm of a used car salesman. Dave winced. That was unkind. Even if it was true. He prayed for patience as he turned.

"Morning, Karl. How's it going?"

"Pretty well. Although, I actually wanted to talk to you about something."

Dave fought not to groan. Conversations with Karl that started out this way were never good. "Oh?"

"I'm moving. Got a job up north and as much as I'd like to do it remotely, it's better all around if I don't."

"Congratulations?"

Karl nodded vigorously. "Oh, yeah, it's a good thing. Big pay raise, lots of perks."

"I'm happy for you. And a little unsure what I can do for you."

"Right. The house. I'm going to sell—I know you do the vacation rental thing when you're out and about, but I just can't wrap my head around that. I mean what if something happens?"

That was what deposits and insurance were for, but renting property also wasn't for everyone. Dave nodded. "The market's pretty good right now, I think. I don't know any real estate agents personally, but I could ask my property manager."

"Oh, no. No, I know someone if it gets to that. I was actually wondering, though, if you might be interested. Why rent one house, when you could have two—that kind of thing. And I notice you've been around a little longer than your usual stopovers, so I thought maybe you were making it permanent. And if that was the case, then there goes your rental income, am I right?"

Is this You, God? You've got a sense of humor, don't You? Karl of all people. "Place needs some work."

Karl's cheeks burned a bright red. He cleared his throat. "Yeah. Obviously I'd knock the price down if you wanted to take that on. You're not saying no outright?"

Dave shook his head. Between Mary's life insurance, a little bit of inheritance she'd had that had rolled over to him, and his thriftiness with rental income and his expenses, he could probably swing it. Maybe. "I'm not. I've got some time—could I come by and give the place a look? I don't think I've ever been inside."

"Sure. Of course." Karl grinned as they turned and started back toward the house. "It's a great little place. Did you know I have a detached in-law suite? I'm using it for storage, mostly. But it could be a pool house—there's a pool, you know—or a separate rental."

Dave nodded, listening with only half an ear as Karl regaled him with all the high points of the house beside his while they walked that way. He'd known about the pool, because Karl tended to have loud pool parties on Saturday nights in the summer. He hadn't known about the in-law suite, and that was an interesting proposition. He didn't need a lot of space—he was one person. A kitchen, bathroom, bedroom, and maybe a little living space and he'd be happy. Which might mean he had two places he could rent. Full time, even, instead of vacation rentals. They were about ninety minutes from Orlando, which made them a stretch for some of the amusement park travelers. But the beach was right here, just across the road, and that was a bonus.

Still, his place would often sit empty in the winter. And there were military families who lived out this way who might think it was worth the extra drive to be this close to the beach.

There were options.

The tour didn't take long, but the state of Karl's house—and the in-law suite was even worse—meant Dave wouldn't be managing two properties immediately. It was livable, though.

"How much?"

Karl's sales pitch broke off mid-stream. "Really?"

"If we can agree on a price. If you're serious about taking the repairs into consideration."

Karl winced, but he nodded. "Between you and me, I don't think I'll buy again. I'm not really Joe Homemaker, you know? I like the idea of a landlord doing all the maintenance and repair."

Dave chuckled. That was obvious from the state of the house. And yet, it was a project he could get his teeth into, and maybe it'd take his mind off Elise. And give him the push to officially retire from the mission agency. "It's not for everyone."

Karl scratched his neck and looked around. He rattled off a number. "That's what I owe on the mortgage. If I can walk away and not be in the hole, I'll be happy."

"I can probably do that." Dave stuck out his hand. "Let me go make a couple of calls and we'll get the ball rolling."

"Just like that?" Karl shook Dave's hand.

Dave nodded. "Sometimes, Karl, God drops something in your lap. And maybe it's not the exact answer to your prayers—or not the way you expected Him to answer, at least—but it's still pretty clearly God at work. When that happens? A smart man doesn't think twice."

"That's how it was with this job." Karl's eyebrows knit together. "It's close to my folks. They're getting up there and I'd feel better being nearby. I don't know about the God stuff, but it seemed like a no-brainer."

"Tell you what. I'll go make those calls. When I'm done, let's go grab some lunch at the Shrimp Shack, my treat, and we'll hammer down the details and talk about the God stuff, too."

"Yeah?" Karl searched Dave's face, then nodded. "Okay."

Dave grinned. "I'll be over around eleven thirty."

"Sounds good. Thanks."

"What would you say if I told you I bought the house next door?" Dave shifted the phone so he could grip it between his shoulder and his ear and free up both hands to open a can of soup.

"I'd say that's a good start at the rest of your life. Did you?" Herb was a steady soul. It was why Dave had called his cell, and not the phone he and Margaret shared.

"I did. On Monday. Well, I started the paperwork Monday. I think we'll get all the signing done sometime next week. Karl's moving up closer to his parents. As soon as he's out, I think I'll move myself next door and get this place listed on a full-time basis." His heart lurched, just a little, at the thought. He and

Mary had bought the house with the intention of growing old together in it. But he was only moving next door. And Mary wasn't here, anyway. He dumped the soup in a bowl and stuck it in the microwave. "There's a lot of work to do on the new place."

"It could use a good coat of paint on the outside."

Dave laughed. "Among other things, yeah. Don't imagine you and Margaret want to come down and help?"

"Maybe after Christmas. Think there'll still be work to do then?"

"I'm fairly certain there'll still be work to do in July. I'm just one man, and I have this idea that I'll do most of it myself. I've got nothing but time."

"What if the board needs you?"

"They won't." Dave sighed. "I sent my official notice of retirement on Monday, too."

There was a long pause before Herb finally asked, "How are you feeling?"

The microwave beeped. Dave popped the door open but left the soup inside. Instead, he wandered to the sitting room and lowered himself into one of the chairs. "I don't know. A little empty inside, I guess. But I know it's the right thing. I guess I knew before you and Margaret came to give me a kick in the pants."

"I'm not going to apologize for that. But I am sorry you're hurting."

"No, I'm not. Change is hard. And I'm old, which makes it harder."

Herb laughed. "You're not old. You're barely past middle age."

"I feel old, then." Dave leaned his head back and let his eyes drift closed. "Still, I have a project. This house will, hopefully, be a good enough income to cover the payments and repairs next door. And if not, I have some savings and Mary's insurance."

"Have you heard from Elise?"

"No." He made himself stop there. He didn't want to get into a conversation about reaching out and making the first move and all the same things they'd rehashed too many times to count when Herb and Margaret had been in Florida.

"Okay. I guess I don't have to tell you what I think?"

"You really don't." Dave sighed. "We'll see, okay? Now that I've made two major decisions to completely change the course of my life, maybe I have the gumption to try again. Or maybe those two decisions are enough."

"What are you hearing when you pray about it?"

"Wait." At least, that was what Dave was interpreting the silence as. He certainly didn't feel any heavenly pushes to pick up the phone and call her. But he got plenty of nudges to pray for her—and so he did. Constantly.

"Then that's what you should do. I'll keep praying He'll make it clear."

"Like He did with the house."

"Oh, yeah? That's a story I want to hear."

Dave summarized the meeting on the beach with Karl and the quiet but steady knowledge that it was the right thing. "So, yeah. If God wants to make the thing with Elise that obvious? I'd be open to it."

"And if He doesn't?"

"I'm still open to figuring it out. I miss her, Herb. It's ridiculous, because we were only together not quite two months. But I miss her almost the same as I miss Mary." Dave rubbed the center of his forehead and prayed again for clarity. None of this made sense, and he needed it to. Why would God allow him to develop feelings like this if Elise wasn't going to reciprocate?

"Want my best advice?"

"Always."

Herb chuckled. "Keep praying and get that house on the

rental market. The more work you do before Margaret and I can come out, the better vacation we can all have together when we do."

"All right. Thanks. I'll talk to you later." Dave ended the call and stared at his phone. He could text her. Again. Or call. But nothing had changed. So why would she answer now when she hadn't been willing to before?

No, it was better to leave things alone. He'd get over her eventually. Or God would bring her back into his life.

Either way, Dave needed to work on being content with the new situation he was in. Whatever else God brought his way would be enough.

21

"I found the perfect place, Mom." Skye's voice burst with excitement and she bounced up and down.

Elise looked away from her computer screen. "Stop. You're going to make me seasick."

"Sorry. I'm just so stoked. It's a great place. You'll love it."

"I guess I'm confused." Elise looked around the living room floor of the stone tower. She liked it here well enough, too.

"Didn't you tell me two weeks ago that you were going to Florida? To the beach? That you needed a change of scene?" Skye frowned at her mom through the video call. "Or was I hallucinating?"

"Watch it, young lady. I'm still your mom." Elise sighed. "But yes, I did say that. Then I changed my mind."

"Why?"

Elise shrugged. She couldn't put her finger on it. "Maybe just because it all feels like so much effort. Azure doesn't mind having me here. She says that Deidre's fine with me staying in the tower. So why not?"

"Didn't you tell me part of the reason you left the ranch was because you needed to stop drifting and doing what was easy instead of what you wanted to do?"

Oh, man. Of course, she had a kid who remembered her words and was willing to toss them back in her face. "Well. Yes."

"Has that changed?"

Elise wasn't going to lie, even if she wanted to. "No."

"So go to Florida, Mom. Lie on the beach and get a tan."

Elise laughed. "I don't think it's lie-on-the-beach weather, even in Florida. But I could walk on the beach and collect sea shells."

"There you go."

"But what about—"

"Mom." Skye's voice held censure and her face made it clear she knew just what Elise was doing.

Elise held up her hands. "All right. You're right."

"Good. I'm going to send you the listing. It's perfect. It's about ninety minutes from Orlando, so you don't have to deal with any of that traffic—although it wouldn't hurt you to go on a roller coaster or two."

Elise shook her head. "No thank you. Maybe when the grandkids are all the right age to enjoy and appreciate it, we'll make a big family trip."

"That sounds fun. I'm not sure we'll ever have that age gap though, given that Livvy's already thirteen."

That was a point. "Fine, when a few more are old enough."

"Okay. Check your email."

Elise used her phone to open the listing. She swiped through the photos of the two-bedroom cottage. "It's lovely. But it's more than I need. I could just get a hotel. One of those extended stay places."

"The beach is across the street. Come on. And, I checked—this is actually cheaper if . . ." Skye pressed her lips together.

Elise studied her daughter on the laptop screen. "If?"

"Well, it's a vacation rental, but the owner is also open to longer rentals. Including short-term ones. Like three or six months." Skye bit her lip. "Don't be mad."

"I'm not mad. That's more what I'm looking for, isn't it?" Elise rubbed her neck. How did her daughter know her better than she knew herself?

Skye nodded. "You don't want the jet set life. You just don't like feeling tied down. But I also think if you found the right place, you'd be happy to settle there. So if you did say a three-month lease and decided you loved it, you could switch it to six months or a year."

"A year." Elise swallowed. "I always figured I'd go back to Hope Ranch."

"Do you want to? Like to stay?"

Didn't she? The idea of the beach—the ocean and the waves—was much more appealing. The ranch had her kids and Betsy and Wayne. A lot of the people she loved. But she could visit—and that might make the time together even more special. "I guess maybe not. I just figured I should."

"Don't do that, Mom. Don't do the 'should' thing. Do what God's prompting you to do. Up to and including calling Dave."

"Oh. Well, I think that ship has sailed, honey. But this beach house looks perfect. In fact," Elise looked up and studied her daughter's face, "if you don't think your siblings would mind, I might just go straight for the six-month rental. That should be long enough to know for sure."

Skye grinned. "They're not going to mind. We all want you to be where God wants you."

Elise nodded slowly. She'd take a day to pray about it and be sure, but it felt right. For the first time in a while, this seemed like the direction she should go. "I appreciate that. You know I want the same for you, right? For all of you."

"We know. Make the reservation, okay?"

"Tomorrow. I'm going to pray some—because I don't like jumping in, and also because I know that's what I ought to do."

"Fair enough. Love you. Text me, would you, after you make the reservation?"

That was an odd request. "Don't you trust me?"

"It's not that."

Whatever. It was an easy enough thing to do. "Yes. I'll text you after I make the reservation. Give everyone my love, okay?"

"Will do. Bye." Skye's face disappeared.

Elise pulled the link up on her laptop so she could see the photos on a larger screen. If she could design a perfect beach cottage, this would be it—down to the distressed wood accents and jars of sand and shells decorating the space. Her heart yearned to be there.

She hovered over the reservation button for a moment before moving the mouse away. She'd told Skye she was going to spend time praying about it, so that was what she'd do. There was no urgency. Other than the realization that she wanted to be near the ocean. That was new. And pressing. But one more day wasn't going to change things.

Her gaze flickered to the property listing agent's name. The fact that Skye—all of her children, actually—kept slipping Dave into conversation made her suspicious. But why would he have a house in Florida when he spent his life traveling around from jungle to jungle? Anyway, the name was decidedly feminine. So she put that out of her mind. Hopefully, they'd all learned that their matchmaking hadn't worked and were willing to just let it go.

Elise left the website open and stood, pacing to the window to stare out across the grounds of Peacock Hill. Coming here had been the right decision. Leaving now was, too. She was much more settled. More able to focus on living out whatever days God gave her and focusing on her family and His calling.

Maybe she wasn't sure exactly what that call was yet, but she didn't have to know. She had income. She had family. A soft place to land if something went wrong. And for now, with the prospect of the beach ahead of her, an adventure in the wings.

So even if she wasn't booking that reservation yet, she could start to pack. If that rental fell through, well, she'd find another one.

~

"You're sure you don't want to wait until after Thanksgiving? It's just two more weeks." Azure leaned against the driver's side door of Elise's station wagon. "I don't like how impulsive this feels."

Elise laughed.

"What?"

"Oh, honey. Think about who you are."

Azure's cheeks reddened. "People change. Grow up."

"I know they do. And you have. And it's right for you and where you are in your life. Just like this is for me." Elise held out her arms. Azure stepped into them. Elise hugged her oldest child and breathed in the wash of memories that came. "You're happy here, right in the middle of God's will for you."

"I am. I've liked having you here, though. Don't stay away so long. Okay?"

Elise stepped back, her lips curving up. "Why don't you all plan to come visit me at the beach? I'll have plenty of room—and if not, I think there are other vacation rentals nearby. Maybe get a break from the January weather?"

"That sounds like a plan." Azure leaned in and kissed Elise's cheek. "Drive safe."

"I still have the group text going with you all—I'll keep you posted. Promise." Elise fought a chuckle, despite how amusing it was that her children had reversed the roles on her. She appreciated the concern, though. "But I should get going. I'd like to make it as far as I can before supper, or thereabout."

"You're not going the whole way?"

"No. I'll stop near Jacksonville. Ish. The rental agent isn't expecting me until tomorrow, anyway."

Azure nodded and opened the door.

Elise climbed in, checked her mirrors, and fastened her seatbelt. "Thanks for having me for so long. I love you."

"Love you, too, Mom." Azure shut the car door and stepped back, crossing her arms over her stomach.

With a smile, Elise eased out of the parking spot and down the gravel driveway that took her past the little cottage where Anna and Duncan lived. The gardens around their place were an explosion of life, even in November. If the cottage had a thatched roof, Elise would have said it could be in Ireland. She hadn't gotten to know the couple super well while she'd been here—they were busy with their landscaping business. And Azure had mentioned their heartache and inability to have children. It made sense, somewhat, that they weren't in a hurry to get close to a woman who'd had five. She said a quick prayer for them as she drove past and made a mental note to keep doing that.

Before long, she was driving around the side of Peacock Hill itself—a gorgeous stone mansion with towers that speared up on either side. It was like something that should be in Italy, not the foothills of the Appalachians, but it somehow worked. Maybe because Deidre and Jeremiah, Claire and Danny, and Matt and Azure had filled it with so much love. Love that extended to the caterers and wedding planners and all the others who came there. Peacock Hill changed people. Just like Hope Ranch did.

Both had made an impact on Elise.

She thanked God for it.

When she reached the bottom of the driveway, Elise stopped. She glanced at her phone as it displayed the left turn that would take her down the mountain and over to the highway. Before she could overthink, she tapped her contacts, scrolled to Dave's, and hit Talk.

As it rang, she turned onto the winding, two-lane road.

"Hello?" Dave's voice was full of hope.

Elise's eyes filled and she blinked rapidly to clear them. "Hi, Dave. It's Elise."

He chuckled. "I saw that. I'm glad you called. How are you?"

"Okay." She paused, nodding to herself. It was actually true —she was okay. It had been too long since that was reality. "What about you? How's Brazil? And I guess I'm also stunned that the reception's so clear."

"You didn't listen to my messages."

She frowned, slowing as she reached the stoplight at the bottom of the mountain. She hadn't, but how would he . . . oh. "You're already back."

"I am. Have been for a while. They only needed me for about a month."

"Well, that's good. When do you leave again? That's a long time for you to be around, isn't it?" Elise turned when the light changed to green, and switched lanes to be ready for the highway on-ramp. She was trying to play it cool, but his voice hurt her heart. She wanted to see him. To hold his hand. For him to finally kiss her. She wanted those things as much as she wanted the beach. But only her location was something she could control.

"There's nothing on the schedule right now. How's the ranch?"

Elise merged onto the highway with a nervous giggle. "I'm actually traveling right now. I came out to visit Azure in Virginia and now I'm on my way to Florida. I miss the beach."

"You like the beach?"

"I do. We—well, I—lived near the coast for several years when the kids were little. We parked the bus at an RV campground and Martin went off to his jobs, and women, around California. But I have a lot of good memories that involve the ocean." She sighed. It was more than that drawing her to Florida, but she wasn't sure she could explain.

"Mary loved the beach. I think she would have liked you."

Elise swallowed. Every time he talked about Mary, she felt like she would have liked to have known her, too.

"Sorry. I talk about her too much, don't I?"

"No. Please don't think that. I don't. You loved her, and it shows, and I think that's wonderful." Maybe it made her a little jealous, but that was understandable, wasn't it? Especially when she hadn't had that kind of love with her own husband. Martin had loved her in his way. And she him. But Elise was starting to realize how much more there was—and she craved it deep in her soul.

"I did." He was quiet a moment. "Your marriage was different."

She laughed and glanced down at her speed, easing her foot off the accelerator so it was closer to the right side of the limit. "Starting with the whole it-wasn't-a-marriage thing."

"Right."

"How much does that bother you?"

"A little, if I'm honest. But neither of you were believers, right? So, that helps somehow."

Elise hummed. "I know I wasn't. I'm not sure about Martin. It's one of the things that bothers me. Having spent time with Betsy and Wayne, knowing how he was raised, how they say there was a time when he embraced Jesus wholeheartedly makes it hard to reconcile the man I knew."

"I imagine it does."

"No answers?"

"Nope. Sometimes, we have to find a way to accept that God's the only one who knows our hearts. And He's the one in charge of determining whether or not someone was a believer. After a while, it's a relief. I'm only responsible for living my life in His will and doing my best to be a consistent example of His gospel. Everything else is up to Him."

"I like that." Elise shifted into the middle lane to avoid a slow-moving semi. "I certainly have enough work to do on my own heart. I owe you an apology. I'm sorry I shut you out."

"I forgive you."

"Just like that?" It shouldn't surprise her. Betsy and Wayne were quick to forgive, too. Like Jesus.

"Just like that. I'm sorry that I didn't make time to tell you sooner about the change in plans. I know dropping it on you like that was wrong."

"Not wrong. Just hard. But it was going to be hard no matter what, and I'm not sure that knowing sooner would have changed anything. I needed to do this—to leave the ranch, visit Azure, figure out that I could be someone other than the mother of Martin's children. And now I have the courage to try out the beach and see if I can make a home for myself—one that's entirely of my choosing."

"I'll be praying for you."

"I appreciate that." She bit her lip and checked her mirrors. "Do you think we could talk on the phone now and then? Maybe . . . maybe down the road you might want to come visit me in Florida?"

"I'd like all of that. I miss you. I've talked myself out of getting on the first flight to Albuquerque too many times to count. I guess that's good, since you weren't there."

She laughed, but her heart warmed. "From what I gather,

Orlando's your better option now. And I'd love to see you, whenever you can make time."

"Will you head back to the ranch for Thanksgiving? Or to Virginia?"

"No." Elise hadn't realized she'd made that decision until she spoke. It felt right. "No, I'm going to give it a shot on my own. I don't think I'll bother with a turkey, but maybe a nice grocery store rotisserie chicken will be good enough."

"Would you like company?"

"You'd do that? Come to Florida for Thanksgiving? You're sure you'll be in the country?"

"I'm sure. I've retired, completely, from the mission agency."

She blinked. He'd retired? Because of her? She didn't ask—didn't dare to hope—but why else would he make that kind of drastic change? "Oh. Then yes. I'd love to have you. And maybe I can put something a little fancier together. I'm certainly game to try."

"I won't complain, but if you wanted to go out, I'd be fine with that, too. I still owe you a fancy dinner."

Nerves jittered in her stomach. Maybe they hadn't lost all the ground she'd thought they would. "What if we saved that for a different day while you're visiting? Can you stay a while?"

"I'll stay as long as you'd like."

"Okay." Her heart pounded in her chest. "I won't get to my rental until tomorrow. But once I'm settled, I'll call you and we can figure out the details?"

"I'd like that. For now, why don't I let you go so you can focus on driving?"

"Probably smart. I'll talk to you tomorrow."

"You will. Be safe."

The call ended.

Elise pressed a hand to her chest and took a deep breath. She'd thought—well, she'd thought so many things. None of them appeared to be true. She breathed out a whispered, "Thank You, Jesus."

She hadn't been in charge of a real Thanksgiving meal in a few years. Martin hadn't cared once the kids stopped coming home. It mattered this year. It mattered a lot.

The minute she was settled in her hotel tonight, she was going to search out recipes that would knock Dave's socks off. And maybe get him to finally kiss the cook.

22

The sun was setting.

Dave peeked around the side of the house he'd bought from Karl to check that the coast was clear before dashing across the road to the beach. The woman who managed his rental listing had texted him as she was leaving the cottage after having shown Elise around, gotten the paperwork signed, and handed over all the keys. So he knew she was here.

It had taken everything in him not to march next door, knock, and wrap her in his arms. But timing mattered, too.

He'd gone back and forth with Skye about his plan. She wanted him to prolong the mystery of where he was—but it seemed entirely too much like lying. He'd sidestepped a few times on the phone yesterday, and that was already too much. He didn't want a relationship built on anything other than honesty.

He doubted Elise did, either.

Finally, Skye had caved and agreed to do her part.

Dave checked the time. He had another fifteen minutes or so to get everything set up. He took a few steps away from the path that led from the cottages and found a quiet stretch of beach that was out of any evening walking traffic that might start. The people who lived here loved the beach and took every opportunity to stroll on it.

As they should.

He just didn't want them kicking sand into his romantic picnic.

He spread out a tablecloth and weighted the corners before stabbing a couple of bamboo patio torches into the sand and lighting them. It wasn't dark enough that they added to the ambience yet, but if all went well, they'd be an asset.

Dave left the food in the picnic basket and tucked his hands in his pockets as he looked over the setup. Should he have done more? That fancy restaurant, maybe? No. This was better.

His phone buzzed and he slipped it out. It was a text from Skye letting him know Elise should be on her way to the beach.

Nerves jangled.

He shifted so he could watch the path. His breath caught as she appeared—pausing when she reached the sand to step out of her shoes, bend to pick them up, and then laugh as she walked toward the water. He watched her a moment before heading that direction.

Elise had stopped just at the edge of the wet sand. Waves came up and lapped at her toes. She had her face tipped up, eyes closed.

"Hi."

She jolted, her hand flying up to her heart.

He smiled.

"Dave?"

He nodded.

"But—already? You came so fast?" Confusion clouded her eyes.

He reached up to rub the back of his neck sheepishly. Here

was where he'd find out just how mad she was going to be. "I actually live in Florida."

"You live . . ." She frowned at him. "Why didn't you say something?"

He didn't really know how to answer. "It never seemed to be the right time."

She shook her head. "I don't understand."

Dave offered his hand and held his breath. Would she take it?

Slowly—too slowly—she reached out and curved her fingers around his.

He breathed out and squeezed her hand. It was familiar, but also exciting. Such a strange dichotomy to have the sensations of school-boy love mixing in with his more experienced heart. And still, at the end of it all, she *was* home. Just like Mary had always been.

"Mary and I bought a cottage here in Florida when we came back to the States. We were close enough to Orlando that we could get to her doctor appointments, but far enough away that we could be near the beach and away from reality."

Elise nodded.

"When she died, I kept the cottage—I needed a home base for the weeks here and there when I was in the country and not running a camp. The rest of the time, I let a property management company deal with it as a vacation rental. I didn't mind the extra income, and I couldn't bear to part with the house." He held her gaze and nodded when her mouth formed a little "Oh."

"You own the cottage I'm renting."

He nodded.

"How . . .?"

"Skye."

Elise laughed. "Of course, Skye. That girl."

"Are you angry?"

She sighed. "No. Not really. This is what I wanted. What I want."

Dave lifted their joined hands to his lips and kissed her knuckles. "Would you like to take a little walk?"

"On the beach at twilight with the man I love?" Elise turned and met his gaze. "Absolutely."

His heart jolted. Had she just said she loved him? She had, hadn't she? "I'm glad you're here."

Her smile faltered.

Dave lowered his forehead to hers. "I love you, too."

"You do?"

He nodded. He watched as her tongue darted between her lips, and yearned to kiss her. Not yet. Slow. They should still take things slowly. "Let's walk a little."

"Okay." She sounded a little off. Was she still wrapping her head around him being here? The cottage? Her daughters and their matchmaking efforts?

"Your girls wanted me to stay out of sight a little longer and just talk on the phone. But I didn't want to lie to you—I don't ever want to lie to you. I want this relationship to grow and be strong with a foundation of trust and honesty."

"I'd like that, too. My girls read entirely too many romance novels these days. Jade is a virtual assistant for some Christian writers. I'm not completely sure it's been a good influence." Elise looked toward where he'd put out the picnic. "Oh, look at that. Someone's planning a romantic dinner."

"Should we go check it out?" He tugged her hand and started on a diagonal path toward the blanket.

"Dave. No. Let them enjoy their moment." She squinted into the shadows. "I wonder where they are."

He stopped and pulled her into his arms. "Right here."

"You did this?"

"I did."

"For me?"

"Who else?"

Elise's eyes filled and she blinked and looked away.

"Don't cry." He reached up and brushed a thumb across her cheek. "I never wanted to make you cry."

"They're happy tears." She took a deep breath and eased back, tilting her head up so she could hold his gaze. "Do you ever plan to kiss me?"

Dave let out a bark of laughter. "I thought you might need me to take things slow."

"I really don't." Elise leaned forward until her lips brushed his.

He closed his eyes and held her tight to his body, his fist bunching the back of her shirt as his lips moved over hers.

I have found the one whom my soul loves.

The thought flitted through his mind, and he tucked it away to think on later.

Gently and with regret, he ended the kiss and stepped back. "Are you hungry?"

Elise's eyebrows lifted.

Dave gestured to the picnic blanket. "For supper."

"Sure. This is lovely." Elise glanced at him as she sat. "Romantic."

"I was hoping you'd think so." He settled beside her and opened the basket. He pulled out a container of brie and crackers, then two champagne flutes and a bottle of sparkling apple juice. When the glasses were filled, he offered her one, tapping his against the edge as he did so. "To new beginnings."

DAVE WHISTLED as he unscrewed the kitchen cabinet doors and carried them out to the sawhorses he'd set up on the backyard lawn. The kitchen wasn't terrible, but it needed some freshening. So he'd spent some time on YouTube and figured painting them didn't look too hard. Sanding and such were mostly just elbow grease. He had a lot of that.

And time.

Between the two, he could probably get it figured out. There wasn't a lot of urgency.

If nothing else, it gave him something to do while he waited for Elise to wake up. They'd had such a nice time on the beach last night. Neither of them had wanted to go back home. Finally, the breeze off the water made it cool enough that they'd had to give in.

Then there'd been that one, lingering kiss at her front door.

He sighed and went back to the kitchen so he could set to work with the drill to get a few more of the doors taken off.

"Knock, knock?"

"It's open! I'm in the kitchen." Dave set down the power tool and dusted off his hands.

Elise wandered in. She held a foil-covered dish and looked around, interest clear in her expression. "This is . . ."

"You can tell the truth and shame the devil." He laughed. "I believe 'interesting' is the polite word."

"You don't live here."

"Oh, I do. But I'm not responsible for it being this way. My neighbor, Karl, wasn't much for home maintenance it turns out. But in the end, that worked to my advantage. Now I have a project and, when I'm finished, new digs plus a second rental property."

"How do you get both?"

Dave nodded toward the dish in her hands. "If I show you, do I get to know what's in there?"

Elise grinned and set the dish down on the island. She peeled back the foil to reveal cinnamon rolls swimming in thick, white icing. "I saw this recipe when I was digging around for something to impress you with at Thanksgiving and wanted to give them a try. I was thrilled to see you keep your rental well stocked."

"I don't, normally. But since it was you, I laid in some supplies—Skye said you liked to bake, so I asked someone at the store about essentials. I didn't want you to have to deal with grocery shopping right off the bat. Not after that long drive."

"Sweet man." Elise reached for his hand. "Why don't we eat, then you can give me the tour."

"I like the way you think." Dave turned and frowned at the empty cabinets. He hadn't put any furniture in the main house. He'd set himself up well enough in the in-law suite, since it should meet all his needs. "Actually, why don't we grab those and I'll show you where I'm living. I'll make this main house into a rental—or, well that was the plan. There's a separate, smaller set of rooms over this way."

"Sounds good." Elise reached for the cinnamon rolls.

"I can carry them." He nodded toward the back door as he picked up the pan. Would she want to live in one of the bigger houses if they married? There was certainly no reason not to. He could still rent the in-law suite—so there'd be two properties. The income would matter more with a wife to support. He glanced at her. Did she know he was thinking this way? He loved her. She loved him. She had to know. Didn't she?

"The pool is nice."

"We can take a swim later, if you want. It's clean and ready for visitors. Karl did keep it up—he was big on morning laps." They crossed the pool deck and on to the pavers that led to the long, low building that sat perpendicular to the main house. He turned the knob and pushed in the door. "After you."

Elise smiled and stepped in. She looked around. "You have two kitchens?"

"This is an in-law suite. When I bought the house, I figured I'd live here and rent the other two. I don't need a lot of space. But now, maybe that needs to change?" He set the rolls down on the small, Formica-topped round table. "Have a seat, I'll get plates."

Elise sat and folded her hands. "It's lovely in here, though. Kind of retro."

Dave laughed. "That's a fancy word for old, right?"

"*Fun* and old though. Vintage is classy, old, and no fun."

He brought the plates and silverware. "So are we retro or vintage?"

"Definitely retro." She used a fork to lever out a cinnamon roll and plop it on one of the plates before repeating the action with the other. Elise pushed a roll toward Dave. "There you are. I tasted the dough last night when I set it to rise, and it was good, but I haven't made these before, and I can't promise anything."

"I'm sure they're fantastic. You want some coffee before I sit down?" Dave jiggled the pot. He'd only had one cup this morning, so there was plenty left. It was warm, but not hot. "I can zap it in the microwave if you want?"

"I'll take some, and I'm sure it's fine as it is." Elise dipped the tines of her fork in the icing on top of her cinnamon roll and touched them to her tongue.

Dave filled two mugs, gathered the sugar bowl and creamer from the fridge, before joining her at the table. It was cozy. Natural. And he yearned for it to never end. "Here we go."

"Thanks."

He took her hand and said a short blessing before letting go so he could dig the side of his fork into the cinnamon roll. It was a good three inches high and still gooey. The smell had his mouth watering before he could get the bite all the way to his mouth. "Heavenly."

Elise's cheeks pinked. She sipped her coffee, not meeting his gaze. "I'll keep the recipe."

"And make it often, I hope."

She reached for his hand.

Dave twined his fingers through hers.

"So you're living here." Elise looked around the space. "Will you freshen it up, too?"

"I was planning on it, but not until after the main house was finished." He forked up another bite of her delectable treat. "There's a sitting room through there, then a bathroom that connects it to the bedroom."

"Clever."

He'd thought so. It made the bath accessible to guests without having to traipse through the bedroom. "It's a little extra privacy, which is nice. Aren't you eating?"

"Hm? Oh. Of course." Elise smiled and cut into her own roll.

"The walls of the living area and bedroom facing the pool and yard are glass. One-way, I think. I need to do a closer inspection, but they have curtains, too. I like all the light, though."

"I wonder why they didn't include that in the kitchen?" Elise twisted to eye the door.

Dave followed her gaze. Sidelights were the only windows—well, and a skylight over the center of the small kitchen space. "I get the feeling the kitchen was an afterthought."

She laughed. "Maybe you're right."

They talked of other things while they finished eating, then, after setting the dishes in the sink, Dave gave her a tour of both houses.

They ended up back in the kitchen he was renovating.

"I'll let you go." He didn't want to, but he didn't expect her to spend every minute of every hour with him. Not yet. "I imagine you have things you wanted to do."

"There's some spinning I should get started on." She held his gaze a moment then added, "What if I brought you lunch, say around twelve thirty, and then after we could take a dip in the pool?"

"I'd like that." Dave stepped closer and wrapped her in his arms. "I'd like that a lot."

23

E lise checked her hair in the mirror one last time. She drew in a deep breath and blew it out, imagining her nerves going with it. There was no reason for them. In the almost six weeks that she'd been in Florida, she and Dave had fallen into a comfortable routine. Most days, she took over breakfast. They'd eat by the pool or in the kitchen of the in-law suite if it was chilly. Sometimes she'd help with a project for an hour or two if he needed a second pair of hands. Otherwise, she'd head back to her place and spin or catch up on email. Or just read a book.

They shared lunch and dinner duties—taking turns, depending on who was in the mood to fix something or whether one of them had unearthed a recipe they wanted to try.

Sometimes they'd go out. There were a hundred little beach-shack restaurants with the most amazing seafood caught fresh that day. They weren't fancy—and they never had managed the fine dining Dave was convinced he owed her—but they were delicious.

And she was with Dave.

That was all she really cared about.

Thanksgiving had been fun. Just the two of them and more food than they'd known what to do with. They'd packaged it up and taken the leftovers to a local soup kitchen. And then ended up signing on to serve meals every Friday.

Now it was Christmas Eve.

They were headed to a candlelight service at their church. Then Dave had said he had something special planned.

Thus the butterflies in her belly.

"He probably means a special dessert. Or a walk on the beach. That's all." Elise brushed at imaginary lint on her slacks, grabbed her purse, and strode out of the bedroom. Enough fussing.

He knocked on the door as she reached the living room. Elise blew out a relieved breath and hurried to it.

"Just in time—" She broke off. Dave wasn't alone. Her kids and their spouses crowded on the front porch with him. Everyone grinned from ear to ear.

"Surprise!" Their voices rang out in a ragged chorus.

"Oh!" Elise clapped a hand to her mouth and stepped back. "Come in! You stinkers."

She hugged each of them as they passed. She and Dave had kicked around the idea of going to the ranch, but decided against Christmas. The snow—neither of them missed it.

Dave shut the door behind him and lifted his eyebrows.

Elise hurried over and wrapped her arms around him. "You wonderful, wonderful man."

"Well, you wouldn't give me any other ideas for a Christmas present, so I had to be creative."

"I love it." She tipped her head back and waited until he met her gaze. "I love you."

His kiss was brief, but tender. "I love you, too. Were you still up for that candlelight service?"

"Of course." She turned and watched as her children, their

spouses, and her grandchildren poked around the house. "Hey, gang. We should get going if we're going to be on time for church."

There were some groans, probably at the thought of sitting more.

"They just came in today?" She looked at Dave for confirmation. He nodded. "Where are they all staying?"

He laughed. "We found a hotel down the road that has suites. Makes it easier and more affordable. Plus it gives the smaller kids a place to nap or just get away from everything if it's overwhelming. They're talking about the theme parks next week —I guess we'll see how that shakes out."

"You didn't pay for this, did you?" There was no way he had the money for this many airline tickets. Let alone the hotels and rental cars.

"Not all. They're pitching in. As are Betsy and Wayne, who sent their regrets saying someone ought to be at the ranch to keep an eye on things." Dave rubbed the small of her back. "Worried?"

"Maybe a little."

He kissed her again. "Don't be."

That was good advice. She watched as everyone filed back out to their cars. Her heart was full. This was exactly what she needed. And everything she wanted. Her gaze cut over to Dave.

Well, almost everything she wanted.

But maybe she was being impatient.

BACK IN THE car after the service and a rowdy dinner at a local seafood place, Elise eased her feet out of her pumps and sighed as Dave started the engine and pointed the car towards home.

"Happy?"

She looked over, smiling. "So happy."

"Tired?"

She shook her head.

"The kids mentioned they'd like to see the beach before they head back to the hotel. That work for you?"

"Of course." Elise was always up for a walk on the beach. And walking on the sand in the moonlight on Christmas Eve with the man she loved? That was even better. Having her children and grandchildren there, too? The best.

"Then that's what we'll do. And tomorrow, they promised to hit the hotel breakfast before descending *en masse* to plan out their week in Florida. So if you have things you've wanted to do, but haven't gotten to, it'd be good for you to have that list handy."

Elise nodded. "I can't think of anything off the top of my head."

"No roller coasters?" He chuckled and made the turn onto their street.

White lights outlined the roofs and porches on their houses. More strands wound around the palm tree trunks. It was a different look for Christmas, for sure, than any she'd had before. But she loved it.

"Maybe. If you're going, I'm going to go, too. And there are always the spinning teacups. Those sound fun."

Dave gave an exaggerated shudder. "Oh, no. Not those."

Elise chuckled. "If you do those, I'll let you choose a coaster. Just one."

"All right. Deal." He steered into his driveway and turned off the car. "Do you want to go in and change or anything before the beach?"

Elise glanced down at her clothes and shook her head. "No. This is fine. It's all washable."

"All right. Onward." Dave pushed open his car door.

Elise followed suit. Dave was always happy to come around and get her door—and most of the time, she let him. But she didn't want to wait with her kids here, and it seemed silly.

He came up beside her and slipped his hand in hers. His voice was loud enough to carry to the whole crew. "It's just this way—across the street then down a little path. You might leave your shoes in your cars if you don't want a lot of sand."

Without checking to see if they were following, Dave and Elise crossed the street and started toward the beach. He led her down to the water's edge. The waves, colder than she'd expected, lapped at her toes. The moon above was bright in a clear sky. A few stars twinkled overhead.

Elise sighed, content, and wrapped her arm around Dave's waist. "This is pretty close to heaven."

He brushed a kiss across the top of her head. "It is."

She felt him shift, twisting to look over his shoulder. "Did they make it?"

"Maybe you should turn around and see."

Elise frowned, but turned.

There was her family, standing in a line. Some held kids who sleepily rubbed their eyes on their hips. Others held sparklers, shooting off white and yellow sparks into the night and illuminating the long roll of paper that had to have been painted by Azure.

The border was awash with color, highlighting swirly letters that filled the center and spelled out, "Will you marry me?"

"Oh." Elise's eyes filled. She pressed a hand to her chest and turned. Dave was on his knee with a ring box in his hand. "Oh you marvelous man, yes."

Dave tried to stand, and laughed. "I'm going to need a hand, I think."

Chuckling while tears spilled down her cheeks, Elise

reached for his hand and helped him up. He took the ring, a circle of channel-set colored stones, and slid it on her hand.

"I love you, Elise Hewitt. Thank you for giving me a reminder that there's still plenty of life left to live."

"Oh, Dave." She might have said more, but his mouth descended on hers and her kids let out a raucous cheer that startled one of the toddlers and set them wailing. Her lips curved as they kissed.

If she had said more, she would have thanked him for giving her a reason to hope.

At last.

∾

A NOTE FROM ELIZABETH...

There's nothing more satisfying than a big, happy ending. Elise finally has the love of a man who respects and cherishes her. More importantly, she and all her kids have come to know the saving love of Jesus.

If you enjoyed Elise's visit to Peacock Hill and haven't spent time in the Blue Ridge Mountains with Deidre and the gang yet, you can begin that series with A Heart Restored, book 1 of the Peacock Hill series.

ACKNOWLEDGMENTS

The end of a series is always bittersweet. I have so enjoyed my time at Hope Ranch and I loved getting to know the Hewitt family better as I wrote their stories. At the same time, I'm looking forward to new adventures and new stories with new characters who are, at this moment, just the barest wisps of ideas in the back of my head.

I'm so very grateful to my husband and boys for not only giving me time and space to write, but for their support and encouragement and hugs. To my sister, who reads my books even though romance is absolutely not her preferred genre. Thanks, as ever, also go to my writer bestie, beta reader, and friend extraordinaire, Valerie Comer. And to the rest of my little Author Tribe - I couldn't do it without you.

And to my readers, thank you. None of this makes any sense without your willingness to hop inside the stories in my head and come along for the journey.

Finally - first, last, and everything in between - thank you to Jesus. For stories, for love, for salvation. For everything.

WANT A FREE BOOK?

If you enjoyed this book and would like to read another of my books for free, you can get a free e-book simply by signing up for my newsletter on my website.

OTHER BOOKS BY ELIZABETH MADDREY

So You Want to Be a Billionaire
Coming soon, beginning summer 2021
So You Want a Second Chance
So You Love to Hate Your Boss
So You Love Your Best Friend's Sister
So You Have My Secret Baby
So You Need a Fake Relationship
So You Forgot You Love Me

Hope Ranch Series
Hope for Christmas
Hope for Tomorrow
Hope for Love
Hope for Freedom
Hope for Family
Hope at Last

Peacock Hill Romance Series
A Heart Restored
A Heart Reclaimed
A Heart Realigned
A Heart Redirected
A Heart Rearranged
A Heart Reconsidered

Arcadia Valley Romance – Baxter Family Bakery Series

Loaves & Wishes

Muffins & Moonbeams

Cookies & Candlelight

Donuts & Daydreams

The 'Operation Romance' Series

Operation Mistletoe

Operation Valentine

Operation Fireworks

Operation Back-to-School

Prefer to read a box set? Find the whole series here.

The 'Taste of Romance' Series

A Splash of Substance

A Pinch of Promise

A Dash of Daring

A Handful of Hope

A Tidbit of Trust

Prefer to read a box set? Get the series in two parts! Box 1 and Box 2.

The 'Grant Us Grace' Series

Wisdom to Know

Courage to Change

Serenity to Accept

Joint Venture

Pathway to Peace

Prefer to read a box set? Grab the whole series here.

The 'Remnants' Series:

Faith Departed

Hope Deferred

Love Defined

Stand alone novellas

Kinsale Kisses: An Irish Romance

Luna Rosa (part of A Tuscan Legacy)

Non-Fiction

A Walk in the Valley: Christian encouragement for your journey through infertility

For the most recent listing of all my books, please visit my website.

ABOUT THE AUTHOR

Elizabeth Maddrey is a semi-reformed computer geek and homeschooling mother of two who lives in the suburbs of Washington D.C. When she isn't writing, Elizabeth is a voracious consumer of books. She loves to write about Christians who struggle through their lives, dealing with sin and receiving God's grace on their way to their own romantic happily ever after.

facebook.com/ElizabethMaddrey
instagram.com/ElizabethMaddrey
bookbub.com/authors/elizabeth-maddrey

Made in the USA
Las Vegas, NV
08 March 2021